SEALING A BARGA[IN]

When Alberta Farrow offered Skye Fargo two-hundred dollars to carry a payroll back to her ranch, just a day's ride, Skye shrugged his okay.

"Then it's settled. We have a deal," Alberta said.

"We do. Should we shake on it?," Skye asked.

"I have something better in mind," Alberta said, and her lavender eyes suddenly darkened. She pulled the buttons at the neck of her long nightdress open. The top of the dress fell away and she moved her shoulders with a little wriggling motion. The nightdress fell to the floor. Alberta faced him absolutely naked, her eyes glinting like tiny, dark pinpoints. Skye stood for a moment and let his gaze drink in the luscious sight before him.

A pocketful of hard cash and his arms full of this deliciously soft-looking body—it was the best deal Skye had made in a long time. He just wanted to do one thing to top it off—teach this range-boss lady who was boss in bed. . . .

Exciting Westerns by Jon Sharpe from SIGNET

THE RANGE KILLERS

by
Jon Sharpe

A SIGNET BOOK

NEW AMERICAN LIBRARY

Copyright © 1985 by Jon Sharpe

The first chapter of this book previously appeared in *The Grizzly Man*, the fortieth volume in this series.

SIGNET, SIGNET CLASSIC, MENTOR, PLUME, MERIDIAN AND NAL BOOKS
are published by New American Library,
1633 Broadway, New York, New York 10019

First Printing, May, 1985

1 2 3 4 5 6 7 8 9

PRINTED IN THE UNITED STATES OF AMERICA

The Trailsman

Beginnings . . . they bend the tree and they mark the man. Skye Fargo was born when he was eighteen. Terror was his midwife, vengeance his first cry. Killing spawned Skye Fargo, ruthless, cold-blooded murder. Out of the acrid smoke of gunpowder still hanging in the air, he rose, cried out a promise never forgotten.

The Trailsman, they began to call him, all across the West: searcher, scout, hunter, the man who could see where others only looked, his skills for hire but not his soul, the man who lived each day to the fullest, yet trailed each tomorrow. Skye Fargo, the Trailsman, the seeker who could take the wildness of a land and the wanting of a woman and make them his own.

*Iowa, the late autumn of 1861,
between the Big Sioux and Little Sioux rivers,
where men fought for a tomorrow
that seldom came . . .*

1

"You get out of that pond and help me, damn you."

The big man in the cool, spring-fed pond frowned back at the girl atop the roan mare. He saw green-flecked hazel eyes in a pert, pretty face, a short, turned-up nose, full red lips, and dark-brown hair cut short.

"Honey, I just got into this pond. I've been riding a long time, I'm hot, I'm tired, I'm jaybird-naked, and you're plumb crazy if you think I'm coming out just because you come riding down the hillside hollering and giving orders," he said.

"I told you, I need some help and you're the only one around. I've offered you more money than most cowhands make in a month," she said, and the big man noted perky, high, round breasts under the checkered shirt she wore.

"I'm no cowhand and I don't need money so bad I do damn-fool things for it," he growled.

"Stop arguing with me and get out of there, dammit," the girl snapped.

The big man frowned lake-blue eyes at the girl. "Honey, if I come out of this cool water it'll be to dip into a warm woman, not to go chasing somebody I never heard of for reasons I don't know and don't give a damn about," he told her.

"You don't have to know reasons. There'll be four men, and I want to get hold of at least one and I can't do it alone," the girl said as her eyes sent out green-flecked hazel sparks.

"That's your problem," the big man said.

She cast a quick glance back up the low hill that fronted the little pond, returned her angry glare to the man standing waist-high in the pond, his powerfully muscled chest and shoulders glistening. "Haven't you ever heard of helping someone, of doing a good deed?" she said.

"Done my share. Don't need to do any more," he returned.

"Maybe you're no cowhand but you're a damn coward, that's what I think," she flung at him.

"Whatever you say, honey," the big man said, and started to sink down into the refreshing, cool water. He stopped with his eyes just above water as he saw the girl spur the roan mare forward, and he started to rise as she leaned from the saddle and scooped up all the clothes he'd left in a neat stack beside the pond. "Now, you hold on a damn minute," he said.

"Cowards ought to be naked. They only hide behind clothes," she snapped as she sent the roan galloping up the hillside, his clothes under one arm. She'd left only his gun belt with the Colt in it on the ground, he saw.

"Come back here, goddammit," Skye Fargo shouted,

but she galloped away and disappeared over the top of the low hill. He sank back and treaded water in the little pond. "Bitch. Stinkin' little bitch," he bit out as he stared at the top of the hill. He didn't aim to go chasing after her with only a gun belt on. He sank deeper into the cool water and felt the movement of the underground spring under his feet as it pushed water upward.

He turned on his back, floated, and let himself hope she'd come back with his clothes after she simmered down. Goddamn, he swore silently. He had carefully checked the surroundings for signs of Sioux or Iowa, checked for any other hoofprints, and gone over the edge of the pond for grizzly or cougar tracks. But he'd found only a scattering of deer tracks and he'd undressed and looked forward to a refreshing, relaxing hour in the cool water. Instead, she'd burst out of nowhere with her crazy demands. Christ, you couldn't guard against something like that, he told himself as he dived deep into the pond, swam under the surface in the clear, cool water, and finally came up for air. He took a deep breath and dived again, turned, rolled under the surface, and generally imitated an otter enjoying himself. Hell, there was nothing else for him to do. Each time he surfaced, he cast a glance at the top of the low hill to see if she were returning with his clothes, but he saw only the gently waving sweet clover.

He swore silently again, dived angrily into the depths of the clear pond, but when he surfaced, he heard the sharp, popping sounds that meant only one thing: gunfire, from beyond the low hill. He swam to the shore of the pond, listened as another flurry of shots echoed over the hill. A third volley popped in the air and then there was silence. He strained his ears and picked up the faint sound of hoofbeats galloping away. He pushed himself sideways through the water to where his gun belt lay at the edge of the pond and put one hand on the Colt. He rested there, half-in and half-out of the water, and his eyes swept the top of the hill as the hoofbeats faded away. He waited, and apprehension and anger stabbed at him as the minutes grew longer and the girl failed to reappear. He shook his head and blew air from his lips as he continued to wait, but only the sweet clover moved at the top of the hill.

"Damn," he muttered aloud as he pulled himself out of the pond, dripping and stark-naked. Maybe he should've helped her, he frowned in thought. Maybe she went and got herself killed, his clothes still with her. If so, she was probably not too far down the other side of the hill. He picked up his gun belt and strapped it around his naked waist. The late-afternoon sun had already started to dry his wet body and he went over to his horse and climbed into the saddle. The Ovaro moved forward, glistening black fore and hind quarters and pure white midsection gleaming in the sun as Fargo prodded him up the slow hill. Nearing the top of the hill, Fargo slid from the saddle and carefully peered over the crest. Only the gently rolling land and the clusters of slippery elms met his eyes; he rose to his feet. He felt not only naked but foolish as hell. He took the Ovaro's reins and started down the other side of the hill.

He picked up the newly flattened line of grass where the girl had galloped down the hill and followed the trail to a cluster of elms. Scanning the ground, he saw the marks in the soil where she'd dismounted and knelt down beside the lower branches of a tree. He ran his fingers along the side of the branch and saw the powder marks there. She had steadied a rifle on the branch as she fired. His eyes narrowed as he peered beyond the trees. She had to have been shooting at a slightly down-ward trajectory, he noted, into a place bordered by a line of small boulders that rose at the end of a little passage. The riders had come up out of the pass and she was wait-ing to blast them from behind the elms.

Fargo walked down to the spot and saw the chipped pieces of rock where her bullets had slammed into the stones. He examined the ground there and noted it was covered with hoofprints, the first ones leading up from the little passage just as he'd figured. He knelt down, his lake-blue eyes narrowing as they studied the marks on the ground. When he was finished, he had a clear recon-struction of what had taken place.

Four riders had come out of the passageway to reach the place in front of the rocks. The girl had blasted them from the elms on the higher ground. Marks showed that the four riders had milled around in surprise at first, then tried to find cover, and finally fled. Blood spots in two places on the ground told him she had winged at least two, but another set of tracks showed that the four horsemen had raced back the way they'd come. Another single line of hoofprints showed that she had started to give chase but halted, most likely because the four riders had too much distance on her.

He rose to his feet and drew a deep breath. Plenty of signs telling him plenty of things, but not a sign of his clothes. The late-afternoon sun had already dried his body but he was still left naked as a newborn babe. "Dammit to hell," he swore, and pulled himself onto the Ovaro. He turned the horse and took off after the tracks where she'd ridden away. At least she hadn't gotten her-self killed and maybe she'd drop his clothes off some-place. But she had said she wanted to get hold of at least one of the men and she hadn't succeeded at that. Probably still blamed him for that, he pondered, remembering the fury she'd generated. She had doubtlessly ridden away wrapped in her own rage. He tracked her prints down to the bottom of the hill, where they unexpectedly turned northwest.

He turned with the tracks, almost lost the trail in a thick field of tall pigeonberry, but managed to pick it up when the six-foot-high stalks abruptly ended. He followed along a ridge of flatland that suddenly dipped and became a deep sinkhole filled with thick, sucking mud. He stared into the sinkhole where a piece of his shirt and part of one boot still protruded from the gray, gluelike mud. Rage swept after realization: the little bitch had tossed all his things into the sinkhole. He swore silently. He didn't dare try to retrieve anything, not in the entrapping, sucking mud that would pull him in to certain, horrible death. Even if he could pull something out, it wouldn't be wearable. Damn her bitchy little hide, Fargo swore again, and spurred the Ovaro forward. He was tempted to keep following after her, but the sun's red orb nearing the horizon ended the thought. He had to find himself some clothes fast. With early frost the late-autumn nights turned cold within an hour after sundown, nights certainly not made for riding around naked.

He cursed again as he headed the Ovaro north across the flatland, the direction he'd been going when he stopped at the pond. He put the Ovaro into a fast trot, the sun's inexorable downward path toward the horizon a grim reminder of the need to get some clothing. He'd ridden almost an hour when he saw the wagon train, four Conestogas slowly plodding their way westward. He started to race the Ovaro forward, was halfway to the wagons when he reined to a halt. He couldn't ride naked up to a wagon train sure to be filled with women and kids. They might well send a dose of hot lead his way when they caught sight of him. They surely wouldn't welcome a naked horseman riding at them. He couldn't blame them. He grimaced as he turned away and crossed far enough behind the wagons to follow from a distance.

As the edge of the sun began to slide below the horizon line, he made his way through a line of tanbark oaks. By the time he reached the other side of the trees, the sun was more than halfway below the horizon. He pulled the horse to a halt as he saw the cabin dead ahead of him, a long, thick-walled structure with two small pens to one side and a large corral of stake-and-rider fences behind. He stayed just inside the edge of the trees and spotted two youngsters, a boy about nine years old and a girl he guessed to be seven or eight. He watched them push a dirty fat sow into one of the pens and close the gate. As the night darkened, he saw a woman emerge from the cabin. She had dark blond hair pulled up tight atop her head and a work-wearied face that nonetheless clung to a certain handsomeness with good, strong features. Her gray work dress was shapeless yet unable to hide large, deep breasts that swung as she bent over to fill two buckets by a well.

She turned into the cabin with the buckets and Fargo watched for signs of a man. Before darkness settled in she made two more trips out of the cabin for firewood and he saw no man anywhere around the house. His eyes went to a lean-to shed that served as a stable at one end of the long cabin. It held two horses, one a dull brown, the other a speckled gray and a light pony wagon in poor condition. The night descended and almost instantly he felt the temperature drop. In minutes he was shivering. He went into his saddlebag and pulled out the blanket there, dismounted, wrapped it around himself Indian-fashion, and sat down at the edge of the trees. But the night air found its way under the edges of the blanket to stab sharply at his naked body.

A fire burned inside the cabin and she'd lighted a lamp whose glow sent a small yellow square of light into the night through the two bottle-glass windows in the cabin. He glimpsed the children and the woman as they moved past the windows, but he still saw no signs of a man. He decided there was none, not about at the moment anyway. His thoughts were confirmed when it was the woman who came out again to bring in a last load of firewood. She had put on a long blue nightdress, and with the flickering light from inside the cabin behind her she managed to almost look as though she were a young girl. He watched her go back inside and close the door, and his lips pulled back in a grimace.

He wished there had been a man inside. He didn't want to frighten the woman, her being alone with only the youngsters. Nor did he want to draw an instant, nervous reaction that might get him shot. But he had to buy, borrow, or beg some damn clothes. Luckily, most of his money was in his saddlebag. He'd only had a few silver dollars in his shirt pocket, and the letter that had brought him out here into Iowa country. He felt the ground begin to harden as the night frost quickly made its way through the topsoil. When the bottoms of his feet were starting to grow cold, he rose, wrapped the blanket around him, and stepped from the trees into the cleared land around the long cabin. He walked forward and halted at the edge of the perimeter of light cast outside through the cabin windows.

"Hello, inside there," he called out. "Hello."

She took a moment but he saw her head appear at the

window; she raised one arm, cupped her hand against the glass to shut out the firelight behind her.

"Out here, ma'am," he called. "I need some help."

He saw her pull back from the window, disappear, and a moment later heard the bolt latch on the door being slipped open. The door opened a fraction and he saw the barrel of the rifle push out. "Who's there?" the woman called.

He took another step into the light. "Name's Fargo, ma'am, Skye Fargo. I'm alone," he said in an effort to be reassuring.

"And I'm a crack shot," the woman replied. "What do you want, mister?"

He drew a deep breath. There was no smooth way to put it, no way to take the bite out of it. "I want some clothes, ma'am. I'm stark-naked under this blanket," he said.

"You're what?" she questioned.

"Naked, ma'am. All my clothes were stolen," Fargo said.

There was a moment of silence and he thought he caught a note of amusement in her voice when she answered. "Now, that's something different, I'll say. I've had men come here asking for food, horses, a place to sleep, water, and money, but I never had a naked one come asking for clothes," she said.

"There's a first time for everything," he growled.

"Step into the light more," the woman said, and Fargo moved forward. "Drop that blanket," she said.

Fargo felt the irritation inside himself at her tone. "I didn't come here to put on a show, sister," he said.

"Fargo, that's what you said?" she asked.

"That's what I said."

"Well, Fargo, you're in no position to give orders or

play modest. I've a right to see if you're telling the truth," she said.

"Why do I think it's more than that?" he returned.

"Maybe it is, but that's none of your concern. Drop the blanket or hightail it out of here," she snapped.

Fargo frowned at the dim shape behind the rifle barrel pointed at him. He lifted his arms and let the blanket drop to his feet to stand naked with only the gun belt around his waist. "Seen enough?" he rasped, and started to reach down to pick up the blanket.

"No," she said sharply. "Stay right there." He rose, straightened, frowned at the doorway. "I'll say this, you are a big, handsome critter," the woman remarked.

"Goddammit, it's cold as hell out here," Fargo protested. He started to reach down for the blanket again and once more halted at the sharpness of her voice.

"Now so fast, Fargo. Toss that gun belt over here, first," she ordered.

He frowned, hesitated, then unbuckled the gun belt and threw it to the door. He saw her push the door open further as she picked up the gun belt, and he scooped up the blanket and pulled it around his shivering body.

She pushed the door fully open and stepped back inside the cabin. "All right, you can come on in, now," she said, and again he thought he heard a hint of laughter in her voice.

2

As he stepped into the cabin, Fargo saw that she had let the dark-blond hair down. It fell loosely below her shoulders, framing her face, and it made her look ten years younger, he noted. She was a handsome-enough women, he decided, and he saw blue eyes survey him with a spark of amused interest that almost wiped the weariness from her face. More than amused interest, he corrected himself, a strangely simmering glow. His eyes flashed around the long cabin. One-half of it was separated by a thick drape, and he guessed the children slept in that section. A three-step stairs led to a small loftlike area at one side of the half-room he was in.

The woman sat down on a puncheon chair, the Colt held in her hand. "Tell me more about yourself, Fargo," she said. "How'd a powerful, handsome fellow like yourself lose all his clothes? Somebody's husband come home early?" The blue eyes held laughter and he felt the irritation inside himself.

"Nothing so good," he growled. Her eyes waited, questioned, and he decided to tell her exactly what had happened. He threw the words out in quick, terse sentences, and when he finished, the amusement still stayed in her eyes. "I don't see anything funny about it," he growled.

"Naturally," she said as she put the Colt down on a wooden box that served as a table. "I wanted to hear you out. I believe in being careful."

"You can believe me," he muttered.

"I do. Nobody's going to make up a story like that one," she said, and he saw her eyes linger on the chiseled handsomeness of his face, slowly travel down his blanket-wrapped form. "Sit down, Fargo." He lowered himself to the floor and sat cross-legged, the blanket held around him. "My name's Alice . . . Alice Calkin," she said. Her eyes moved down the blanket again. "It's right warm in here by the fire," she remarked.

"Meaning what?" he asked.

"Meaning you can drop that blanket some. You're modest as a schoolboy, aren't you?" she said.

"Being modest's one thing. Being on exhibit's another," he said, but she was right, he was feeling hot under the blanket. He let the blanket drop from his shoulders and it fell to the floor to lay in folds around his pelvis. He saw Alice Calkin's eyes move down the muscled beauty of his body, saw her tongue come out to lick at her lips. "You have any clothes I can wear?" he asked.

"Got a few of my husband's things still in the trunk. Haven't opened it since he died two years ago," Alice Calkin said. "But there's nothing that'd fit the size of you."

"I'd like to try, anyway," Fargo said.

Alice Calkin looked thoughtful. "There's pair of trousers. If I let them out you might just be able to get into them," she said.

"I'd appreciate that," Fargo said.

She nodded but made no move to fetch anything. She leaned back, ran a hand through the loose dark-blond hair, and he saw those deep, heavy breasts push against the blue nightdress.

"I'll pay you for anything I can wear. For your fixing them, too," he offered.

"Don't need money," Alice Calkin stated, and he caught the unsaid in her voice as her blue eyes traveled over his body again. He paused, hesitated for a moment, but the glow in her eyes stayed.

"You need something else, Alice?" he asked.

She pulled her eyes from him with what seemed an effort and stared into the fire. She looked suddenly uncertain, almost saddened. But the flickering light played across her face, let the dark-blond hair take on tiny gleamings. Alice Calkin was a handsome woman he decided again, despite the lines of care that had settled into her face. When she turned her eyes back to him, he saw something close to anger in their blue depths. "You're wondering about me. Can't blame you for that," she said.

"I'm wondering," he admitted. "But you don't owe me any explaining."

"Yes, I do, so you'll understand. Maybe owe it to myself, too," she said, and her face grew solemn. "Two years is a long time, Fargo."

"It is," he agreed. "But there had to be other men come by here."

"Yes, coarse, grubby rangehands, some that worked at Barnaby Tilden's place, men I wouldn't sit down to breakfast with, much less anything else," Alice Calkin said. "Two years and suddenly you're standing there—tall, handsome, your beautiful body naked—and I seemed to explode inside. Two years of wanting, waiting, doing without, Fargo. A dry leaf sets on fire easily. It's ready to burn. A body can get that way, Fargo, can you understand that?"

"I can," he said, and Alice Calkin's lips were parted, her breath coming in a low, hissing sound. He felt a surge of compassion and excitement go through him, one mingled in with the other. A woman eager to burst into flame was always exciting, and Alice Calkin was certainly that. But she was more. She had carried her lot with strength and with her own standards held intact.

"So that's how it is," she said. "That's why I'm set on fire."

"I think I'd be honored, Alice Calkin," Fargo said softly.

Her blue eyes suddenly misted, grew soft. "Thank you," she murmured. Her hand rose, pulled at the drawstring at the neck of the blue nightdress. The garment opened at the neck, grew suddenly loose. As she rose to her feet, she pulled it from her shoulders. He saw her breasts billow out, white mounds of softness, very heavy, very deep, and very round, with large brown-pink nipples and equally large brownish areolas. She stood before him as she had had him stand before her, and his eyes took in full hips with a little extra flesh on them, a belly a little too plump, thighs also carrying a little weight, but it was a mature woman's body, ripe and throbbing. A very curly tangle of black density seemed to reach out of itself and Fargo felt his maleness responding at once. He pushed himself to his feet and the blanket stayed on the floor. Alice Calkin's eyes went down to the swelling, throbbing organ that waved at her. He heard the sharp intake of her breath as he stepped toward her. Alice Calkin started forward, fell to her knees, and threw her arms around his legs as she pressed her body against him, the heavy breasts enveloping his organ.

"Oh, Jesus . . . ah, ah, Christ," she rasped, and pulled him hard against her, moved her breasts back and forth against his organ, and suddenly her hands unclasped from around the back of his thighs and she reached for the throbbing spear. Her hands curled around him and she gasped out a shuddered cry as she held him, eyes closed, as a penitent holds a chalice. Soft, cooing sounds came from her as she clung to him, her eyes staying closed. He reached down, put his hands under her shoulders, and lifted, and she gave a gasp of protest, her eyes snapping open as he pulled from her grip. He moved her to the mattress on the wooden frame against one wall of the cabin, holding her just off the ground, and he let his face push into the heavy, round twin mounds as he gently put her on the bed.

"Oh, yes . . . oh, oh . . . aaaaah . . . aaaah . . ." Alice Calkin half-groaned, half-cried as softness enveloped his face and his lips found one pink-brown nipple and closed around it. "Oh, yes, oh, yes," she murmured as he drew the surface of one soft mound into his mouth. "So long . . . so long," she murmured, and her full-fleshed body rose up and trembled as he sucked and drew on the firm nipple. "God, Fargo . . . God," Alice Calkin cried out, and he felt her hands clutching at him, pulling at him as her legs drew up, soft-fleshed thighs falling outward against his ribs. "Don't wait . . . don't wait . . . go on, go on, Jesus, go on," she cried, and rolled half onto her side as he pushed the dense triangle into him, the portal seeking the key. "Please, Fargo, please," she pleaded, and he heard the urgent wanting in her voice. He rolled over onto her and she half-screamed at the very act, the meaning, the promise. Her full-fleshed thighs came apart, scissored together around him at once. "Yes, yes, yes . . . Jesus, yes," Alice Calkin said, and her plump little belly pumped against him as she lifted, trembled, urged.

He felt her urgency, a passionate contagion, and thrust quickly, harshly, slipped easily into her, and she screamed with pleasure. "Aaaaah . . . aaaiii . . . oh, yes, yes, oh so long . . . so long, please," she cried, words and sounds mingling together. She pumped against him, her round, full rear lifting him as she lifted to meet his every thrust. He buried his face into the twin, pillowy mounds and raised his head to see her arching her neck back, dark-blond hair streaming in an arc against the mattress. He felt her belly grow tight and heard the cry begin deep down inside her. "Oh, God . . . aaaah . . . aaaaaggggg . . ." the cry began, a throaty rumble that became a roar of pleasure, and Alice Calkin's full body came hard against him to push, clutch, hold until, with a rush of breath, she fell back on the mattress and stared up at him. He rested inside her, still throbbing, as her quickness had taken him by surprise. "Stay . . . stay," she murmured. "Do it again . . . now . . . oh, God, I need it again . . . again."

Alice Calkin's hand encircled his neck, pulled his face down onto the deep, heavy breasts, held him there as she half-turned first one way then the other, rubbed the brown-pink nipples back and forth across his face, letting the pillowed mounds all but smother him with sweet suffocation. He caught one tip in his mouth, held, bit gently, and she cried out in pleasure. He felt himself iside her growing stronger again, moving slowly backward and then thrusting in, and Alice gasped out pleas for more. He stayed over her, his body caught her softness; and felt her rounded belly trembling as he moved inside her. Once again, the past allowed her no patient pleasures and she pressed the fleshy thighs around him again, lifted with him, brought her trembling belly hard up against his muscled abdomen as he thrust harder into her.

"Jesus, yes . . . yes, yes . . . oh, more, more . . . oh, Jesus," she breathed between rasps of air as she drove upward with his every thrust. She was large, but flowing so heavily she had become as smooth as a silk glove. He moved back and forth effortlessly until he felt her belly grow tight again and once more she arched her neck backward as she let a shuddered cry spiral from deep inside her. "Oh . . . oh, Jesus," she breathed slowly as she sank back, suddenly depleted, her eyes holding his. "Not just remembering, Fargo," she said. "Not just all the wanting. You, Fargo, you made it all better than ever."

"Maybe." He smiled. "And then maybe it was a little of everything else all come together. You won't know, not ever."

She pushed herself up on one elbow. "I could, if you stayed around, Fargo," she said.

"Sorry," he told her.

Her little smile was rueful. "Didn't expect so," she said.

"I saw two youngsters," Fargo said. "I kept wondering if you were going to wake them."

Alice Calkin smiled. "They sleep hard. They wouldn't wake if the cabin blew up." She rose and pulled the nightdress around herself, and Fargo smiled inwardly, the gesture not made of modesty but the instinctive realization she hadn't the young girl's figure for parading around any longer. "Let me see about those trousers," she said, and Fargo watched as she climbed the few steps to the little loft.

She opened an old trunk, rummaged inside it for a moment, and came back with a pair of trousers and a shirt. The shirt refused to go over his shoulders and the trousers were loose enough in the leg but nowhere else. "There's plenty of material to let out on these," Alice said, and fetched scissors, needle, and thread.

Fargo sat back on one elbow and watched her as she worked on the trousers, cutting away stitching, resewing, fitting, her hands moving with sure deftness. "How do you manage out here all alone, Alice?" he asked.

"Barnaby Tilden sends me his overflow calves and young hogs to raise for him," she said.

"Who's Barnaby Tilden?" Fargo asked.

"His place is up north. He's the biggest breeder of calves and hogs around here, his whole spread's made up of breeding stock," she said. "Barnaby sells his young stock to every rancher, farmer, and homesteader in this part of Iowa. Raising young stock can be a tricky business out here. When they buy from Barnaby Tilden, the hard part of raising's over with."

"And he sends you his overflow," Fargo said.

Alice Calkin's smile was reflective. "Yes, but I know that lots of times he's just doing a good deed to keep the children and me eating. My husband worked for Barnaby Tilden when he died, and Barnaby is a good man who believes in doing the right thing."

"The Sioux leave you alone?" Fargo queried.

"They come by, watch me, and go on. I think they don't know what to make of me and I've nothing they really want," she said.

Fargo made an uncertain face. "You've been lucky. You can't predict what the Sioux will do," he said.

"I know," she admitted. "I'll have enough saved by the end of the winter so's I can move in closer to town." She put down her needle and handed him the trousers. "Try them again," she said, and he rose, pulled the pants on. He could close the waist and the front, though the legs stayed inches short. "Not a tailor-fit but they'll get you to Rock Hollow." She laughed. "Abe Zeiden's General Store will have something to fit you. Just where were you headed when you met that gal?"

"North of Rock Hollow, the Farrow ranch. Know them?" Fargo answered.

"Heard of them. Big cattle ranch," she said.

"Hired me to find them a new trail down into Kansas Territory, Dodge City," Fargo said. Alice leaned forward against him, pressed the pillowed breasts into his chest through the nightdress. "I'll ride on, come dawn, before your young ones wake," he said.

She slipped the nightdress over her head and rested one deep breast into the palm of his hand. "I figure we've six hours till dawn. You could sleep five of them," she suggested.

"Five would be plenty." He grinned and lay back on the mattress. He closed his eyes and she curled herself against him. He settled himself in the security of the cabin and let himself sleep soundly while the glowing fire kept the room warm.

The five hours of good, hard sleep was more than enough for him, and Alice Calkin woke at once as he stirred and sat up with the hour still left before dawn. When the day finally came, it arrived with Alice Calkin's groaning scream of fulfillment. He lay beside her for a few minutes more and then rose and drew on the ill-fitting trousers. She came to him, ran her hands up and down his body as though she were letting fingers store up touch, sensation, memories of the senses. "Maybe you could come back this way, Fargo," she said.

"Maybe," he answered as she pressed the heavy breasts against him. Finally, the nightdress on, she walked outside with him and he pulled himself onto the Ovaro. He rode away in the early-dawn light and heard her close the cabin door as his eyes scanned the terrain. Caution was ingrained in this land where the unexpected all too often meant sudden death. But not always, he smiled as he thought about Alice Calkin. He put the horse into a trot and hurried northward once again.

The sun had come into the afternoon sky when he caught sight of Rock Hollow and rode into the town. He drew a few curious stares as he rode down Main Street bare-chested, and he wondered angrily if he'd ever meet up with the pert-faced girl with green-flecked eyes again. He still owed her and the thought drew his lips together.

Rock Hollow turned out to be a little bigger than most towns, but like others, the two most prominent buildings were a run-down boarding house and the saloon, which sported a weathered sign with a poker hand and a bottle under the name, THE SILVER GARTER. Plainly a gambling saloon along with dance-hall girls, the place seemed noisy and busy as he rode past.

Abe Zeiden's General Store turned out to be only a few doors from the Silver Garter. Fargo dismounted and walked into the store to see a thin, balding man in a white apron look up as he entered. Though Abe Zeiden's brows lifted as Fargo halted before him, he had stayed in business and alive by not asking questions. "Need some clothes," Fargo said.

"I'd agree there," Abe Zeiden remarked, taking in his height and the breadth of his shoulders. "We've got a few things that ought to fit you," the storekeeper said, and led the big man into a rear room. He gestured to a corner. "Anything on those shelves ought to be all right," he said, and returned to the front of the store as a woman entered. Fargo tried on clothing, found enough things that fit, and picked out a good buckskin jacket to go with his shirts and trousers. He paid the storekeeper with money he'd taken from his saddlebag and left wearing a reasonably well-fitting set of clothes. It was time he'd bought himself a new outfit, he admitted silently, but that didn't excuse one sassy little bitch.

He'd reached the Ovaro outside when he saw the crowd of men spill out of the Silver Garter, moving quickly to give room to the two in the center of the crowd. The two squared off and Fargo frowned at the contrast. One man stood at least six feet, a burly, beefy-faced figure with heavy arms. He wore worn range-hand's clothes while the other man couldn't have been more than five feet, five inches, perhaps less, Fargo guessed. He looked the picture of the mail-order-catalog dandy, clothed in a pearl-gray suit with a three-button vest, a silver necktie with a gold stickpin.

Fargo's glance lingered on the little man's face for a moment to take in a rodentlike, sharp countenance, black darting eyes, a long, thin nose, black hair, and a tight-skinned, narrow face. "I'm going to stomp you into the ground, you fancy little shit," the burly man growled. "Nobody orders Butt Macon out of a lousy bar."

The group that had spilled out of the Silver Garter was quickly joined by others that rushed up to see a fight. "Go get him, Butt," a man among the onlookers called out, and the burly man moved forward, his heavy arms half-outstretched, a leering snarl on his beefy face. The diminutive figure didn't move, Fargo saw, but his black eyes darted ceaselessly back and forth. With a half-roar, the bigger man rushed forward, swinging a long-armed blow. The little man moved, stepped to one side lightly as the burly figure followed through with another bull-like rush and a looping left. Again, the little figure moved, prancing little steps that were almost dancelike as he deftly avoided both rushes. The bigger man halted, snarled again as he turned. "I'm going to break you in half, you little pimp," he said, and charged again. Once more Fargo saw the small man lightly avoid the rush.

The man who'd called himself Butt Macon whirled and sent a hooking blow, grunting with the force of the wild swing. It only grazed the top of the little man's head as he dropped down in a loose, supple motion. Macon tried a straight right, which he drove forward with all his weight behind it. Again, the little man deftly avoided the blow. The momentum carried Macon bulling forward, and the little man twisted away with a quick, darting motion; Fargo saw his foot push out, hook around the bigger man's ankle. Butt Macon went sprawling forward to land facedown on the ground.

With a roar of rage, Butt whirled to spring back to the attack, but as he began to push himself to his feet, the little man stepped forward quickly. Fargo saw the black, shiny, polished boot with a pointed toe lash out to catch Butt Macon on the point of the jaw. The bigger man's head snapped back and his eyes went blank as he toppled sideways to the ground. But Fargo saw the little man prance forward again, a quick, agile step, and his arm came down in a sweeping arc. Butt Macon's head suddenly lolled to one side and Fargo saw the slash of red across his throat.

The fight had ended with chilling suddenness, and the little man bent down, wiped a ring on his right hand across Butt Macon's shirt, and Fargo glimpsed the tiny, razorlike blade at the top of it. The diminutive man straightened, his fancy pearl-gray suit hardly ruffled. "Have Sam Johnson pick him up," he said to the onlookers disdainfully and a man beside Fargo stepped back, brushed against him.

"Who's he?" Fargo asked, and nodded toward the dapper diminutive figure.

"Ed Carver. Owns the Silver Garter," the man said. "These damn fools keep trying to take him on because he's so small."

The man moved away as the crowd began to disperse, and Fargo watched a cold, scornful little smile flash across Ed Carver's ferretlike face as he disappeared into the saloon. There'd been no need to kill Butt Macon. The kick to his jaw had ended the fight. The little saloon owner had a large streak of viciousness in him, Fargo decided as he climbed onto the Ovaro and rode out of Rock Hollow, the uncalled-for killing a sour taste in his mouth.

He rode northwest with the sinking sun, following the directions that had been part of the letter. At a snarled, wind-bent hornbeam, he turned left and rode through a small valley, and when he emerged at the other end, the ranch buildings rose up directly ahead. He took in long corrals crowded with steers stretching beyond the main house, which rose higher than the outbuildings, heavy timbers atop a stone base, a house that spelled money and substance. He made his way past cowhands moving steers into corrals, and as he drew up before the main house, a man detached himself from the others and rode up to where he halted. His stare questioned without words.

"Name's Fargo. Abram Farrow sent for me," Fargo

said as he dismounted and took in the man. He saw a face made of eyebrows so thick they seemed to constantly frown, a stolid face with suspicious eyes. The man swung from his horse.

"You the Trailsman?" he questioned.

"Been called that," Fargo said, tried a smile, and received no response.

"I'm Yakes, the foreman here," the man said. "This way."

Fargo followed the man as he turned and went into the house. He found himself in a large living room furnished with heavy, carved pieces, a large round oak table and a dark-red leather couch. The main window of the house looked out over the corrals beyond, and a small stairway led to an upper floor. As had the outside of the house, the room spoke of a quiet richness.

"I'll get him," Yakes said, and disappeared into another room. Fargo perched on the arm of a large, stuffed chair and took in the two, tall porcelain vases that graced the two nearest corners of the big room. Abram Farrow was plainly a successful rancher in a land where most failed. Fargo rose as he heard a sound and saw a figure appear in the doorway. A man moved toward him with an uneven gait and Fargo saw gray-white hair, shoulders that were stooped and drawn together, a face that looked at him out of tired, lined eyes.

"I'm Abram Farrow," the man said. Fargo nodded and saw a wry smile across the man's face. "No need to hide your surprise, Fargo," Abram Farrow said. "I know I'm not what you expected. Most folks react the same way. A damn bull trampled me five years ago, left me all bent up like this."

"Must've been real bad," Fargo said.

"It was, but I came through and I still run the

Double-C, believe me," the man said with too much defensiveness in his voice, Fargo noted. "Glad you made it, Fargo. We'll be ready to drive cattle in a few days over that new trail you're going to find for us. I hear you're the very best," Abram Farrow said.

"I try," Fargo allowed.

"Can't ask more than that," another voice cut in, a soft woman's voice, and Fargo turned to see her come forward into the room, tall, strikingly handsome, a cream-white skin against which very thin, slightly arched brows seemed to be blacker than they were, a thin nose with a slight flare to the nostrils. Black hair worn loosely framed a sharply planed face and eyes the light lavender of rosemary. "I'm Alberta Farrow," she said as she extended her hand.

Fargo saw Yakes move into the room behind her, his stolid face unsmiling, the suspicious eyes intently watching. "My pleasure," Fargo said as he took her hand.

She held his grip for a fraction of a moment longer than necessary and her eyes appraised him with undisguised appreciation. "I didn't expect anyone quite so handsome when I wrote that letter to you," she said, and Fargo's quick glance at Abram Farrow was unplanned.

"My hand's been shaky ever since the accident," the man said. "Alberta does all the writing these days."

Fargo watched Alberta Farrow step to the center of the room. She walked with a slow, undulating movement of her hips, and her dark-green dress hung loosely on her tall figure, which hid what seemed to be slightly long, modest breasts. He guessed Alberta to be in her mid-thirties, some twenty years younger than her husband.

"I told Fargo we'd be ready to drive in a few days," Abram Farrow said to his wife as she paused near him.

"Yes, we should be ready by then," Alberta said, and her eyes went to the big man with the lake-blue eyes. "Yakes will lead the drive itself with you breaking trail. I guess some six more hands ought to be enough," she said. "That's all I can spare at the moment." Alberta Farrow spoke with quiet authority and Fargo felt himself wondering who really ran the ranch.

Abram Farrow's voice cut into his thoughts. "Yakes, turn the young steers out to graze. Let them get some dew on the grass," the man said. Fargo saw the foreman's eyes go to Alberta.

"Yes, do that, Yakes, that's a good idea," she said, and the foreman walked from the room. Fargo nodded inwardly. His question had been answered. "I'll show you the herd, Fargo. We've some time before dinner. You will join us for dinner, I hope," Alberta said.

"I'd be obliged," Fargo said, and followed the woman as she started from the room. He saw Abram Farrow sink into one of the big chairs and seem smaller and more bent in on himself than before. Fargo's eyes took in Alberta's figure as she walked before him. Maybe a little too much rear, he mused, but she walked with a smooth, gliding motion the loose green dress couldn't hide. She led him out to the main corral, which was packed with steers. A cowhand passed, halted, tipped his hat to her.

"Seth Bailey," she introduced. "He's my assistant foreman. He'll be going along with Yakes on the drive."

"Heard about you, Fargo." The man smiled out of a ruddy face with a shock of graying hair. "Hope you can find us a quick and easy trail."

"I'll do my best," Fargo said as the man hurried on.

34

Alberta's eyes went to him and Fargo nodded. "He's a lot pleasanter than Yakes," he commented.

Alberta Farrow's laugh was low, a soft sound. "Yakes is a man who doesn't understand his own limitations," she said. "Men like that are always unhappy."

Fargo smiled at the observation and the unsaid, and let his glance move across the steers in the big corral. "Mostly whiteface, but you've some Texas longhorns mixed in," he remarked.

"The Herefords have been our big market steers. Buyers snap them up. But they're not as hardy as the longhorns and they can go bad in big numbers. We keep the longhorns as backup, sort of market insurance when the herefords take sick on us," Alberta explained.

"Looks to me as though the Farrow ranch is doing right well," Fargo observed.

"Yes, it is, mostly because we're never out of steers for market between the Herefords and the longhorns. Some of the smaller ranches are going in heavily for Herefords, which helps us, strangely enough. It brings more buyers out and keeps them coming. We sell everything we can bring to market," she told him, and he fell in step beside her as she started back to the house and night began to slide over the land. "You'll get a chance to meet Owen and Janet. They'll be at dinner tonight," she said. "It's a rarity to get the whole Farrow family at one meal, and Abram is always so happy when that happens."

"Abram is?" Fargo echoed blandly.

She tossed him a quick glance, the lavender eyes appreciative. "My, you do pick up quickly on things, don't you, Fargo?" she remarked.

"You learn to look and listen for little things when you ride trail," he answered mildly.

"They're Abram's children from his first marriage. Of course, they're no longer children," Alberta said.

"They live here?" Fargo questioned.

"Owen does. Janet has her own place, bought it with money her mother left her," the woman answered.

He slid the question at her. "I've the feeling you don't care much for either of them."

Her smile was coated. "Owen thinks the income from the ranch is his to squander. Janet's got a head full of her own crazy ideas," Alberta said.

"Mr. Farrow agree with you on that?" Fargo asked mildly as they entered the house.

"He's always been too indulgent with them, especially Janet. If it weren't for me, they'd walk all over him," Alberta said, and he heard the note of hardness come into her voice. She paused at the doorway to the living room. "I'll make drinks while you wash up at the end of the hall. You look like a bourbon man to me," she said.

"Bull's-eye," he answered, and she went into the living room as he made his way to the bathroom at the end of the hall. He thought about Alberta Farrow as he cleaned up. It was plain she wasn't being satisfied by her husband and her lavender eyes sent out their own signals. But she was a striking, clever, and strong woman. He'd let her make the first move. He might push her along a little, but he'd let her make it. She was the kind who'd want it that way and he didn't give a damn about that so long as she wound up in bed with him. It was going to be a long, dry run to Dodge City, Alice Calkin notwithstanding. After all, a prudent man stored up on water before setting off over a desert. Why not store up on a little pussy before a drought? He smiled as he returned to the living room. The world turned in unexpected ways. It was almost enough to make him forget about the stinking little bitch who'd left him to freeze his ass off. Almost.

He strolled into the living room and met Alberta Farrow's lavender eyes as she handed him the glass of amber liquid. Abram Farrow had straightened up a few inches in the chair, a glass of whiskey beside him.

"To a successful drive," Alberta said, and raised her glass and her eyes danced over the rim at the big man in front of her.

Fargo drank to the toast and the bourbon was good and rich. He took a long pull and lowered his glass as a young man entered the room, a slight swagger to his walk. Medium height, in his early twenties, Fargo guessed, brown hair hanging carelessly, and he wore a shiny gun belt with a Colt in the holster.

"Owen, this is Skye Fargo," Abram Farrow introduced. The younger man nodded with the kind of politeness that was a dismissal, and Fargo took in eyes too quick to look away, a mouth self-indulgent, almost petulant, a face entirely devoid of any strength.

Owen Farrow perched on the edge of a chair. "They tell me you're real good at breaking a trail," he said. "Sure hope so. The faster we get steers to market, the more we make."

"I understand that," Fargo said.

Abram Farrow's voice cut in. "Where've you been all day, Owen?" he asked, and Fargo saw the younger man's face grow sullen at once. "You been seeing that dance-hall girl from the Silver Garter again?" Abram pressed.

"Who I see is my business," Owen Farrow snapped.

"Putting your time to working around here is my business," his father returned, and Fargo saw he hadn't the strength in his voice to match his words. "What about the deed to that land you bought up Eagleton way?" Abram asked.

"Nothing to worry about, I told you," Owen said.

Alberta spoke sharply. "A two-thousand-dollar loan out of ranch funds deserves a better answer," she said.

"The man's sick. He'll sign in a few weeks. If not, I get the money back," Owen Farrow said with irritation in his voice.

Abram's voice was tired as he cut in. "We shouldn't be airing family squabbles in front of our guest," he said.

Alberta tossed her husband a placating smile, Fargo saw. "No, we shouldn't. That's poor manners. Besides, dinner's ready," she said.

"Janet's not here," Abram said.

"Start without her. She knows what time dinner is," Owen Farrow snapped.

"She does. I'm not waiting on her whims," Alberta agreed, and walked over to help her husband from the chair. She led the way to the dining room, where Fargo saw a long, polished cherry-wood table set with gleaming silver and bone china. Alberta seated herself across from him and a round-bodied, elderly blond woman appeared with the first course of hot beef soup on a silver tray. Abram Farrow questioned Fargo on possible trails south into Kansas Territory and listened carefully to Fargo's thoughts. They had just finished the soup when Fargo heard the footsteps hurrying into the house.

"Janet," Owen said with distaste.

"About time," Alberta sniffed.

Fargo's eyes were on the door as the girl strode in and he heard the sharp intake of his breath as he met the green-flecked hazel eyes in the round, pert face. He was glad to see his astonishment was matched by hers as her mouth fell open and she stared at him. "You!" she breathed. "What are you doing here?"

"This is Skye Fargo, the Trailsman, the man who's going to ride trail for the drive," Alberta answered, and Fargo saw her eyes flick from the girl to him and back to Janet.

"No, not him," Janet said tightly.

"Obviously, you've met," Alberta said.

"We have," Fargo said grimly, his eyes boring hard into Janet Farrow. "You want to tell them?" he asked.

She flashed a pugnacious glance at the others and flung out terse sentences of how she'd come onto him and asked him for help. "It was the four men who'd killed Jeff," she said. "And I needed help to get them."

"Come now, Janet. That again?" Alberta said chidingly, and Fargo saw the younger woman's face redden with anger.

"Yes, that again," she spit back. "I recognized one of them." She turned to fling a glare of fury at Fargo. "But he wouldn't help me. He's a damn coward," she said.

"Only a damn fool would listen to a gal come shouting crazy orders out of the blue," Fargo said.

"Of course, how could you expect anyone to react differently?" Alberta interjected.

"He wouldn't even come out of the damn pond he was so scared," Janet snapped. "He's a damn fraud and a coward."

"Now, hold on, Janet. Fargo has a mighty fine reputation," Abram said.

"Lots of people get reputations they don't deserve. You'd best find someone else for your drive. He wouldn't be worth a tinker's damn if there was trouble," Janet flung back. "And I'm not having dinner with the likes of him."

"Then it's best you leave. I'm not having our guest insulted," Alberta said coldly.

"Doesn't bother me any. I take words from where they come," Fargo said.

Janet's angry eyes swept the others and he saw her high, round breasts press hard against the gray-green shirt she wore as she pulled herself very straight. "You're fools, all of you. You don't want to believe me about anything. You deserve him," she threw at them, and started to spin around. She paused to spear Fargo with the green-flecked hazel eyes. "Coward," she hissed.

"Bitch," he growled. She stalked away, heels clicking across the floor, and slammed the outside door so hard the glasses on the table shook.

"Our apologies for Janet, Fargo," Alberta said. "She's a very emotionally upset woman, as you can see."

"She's got a rotten temper, I know that much," Fargo said.

"My daughter's always been headstrong," Abram Farrow said. "It's worse now. She thinks everyone's against her."

"You can't reason with her. I think she's imagining all kinds of things that fit in with her crazy ideas," Alberta added.

"I'm sick of talk about Janet," Owen interrupted crossly. "Let's finish dinner."

"Yes, of course," Alberta said, and had the rest of the meal served. Fargo admired the smoothness with which she changed the mood and the conversation away from Janet. When the meal ended, Owen Farrow pushed himself from the table at once.

"I thought you'd stay around tonight, Owen," his father said, disappointment in his voice.

"Can't. Got a deal that'll really make us some money when I close it," Owen said.

"And take more money to swing," Alberta sniffed.

"Any good deal takes investment capital," Owen returned as he started from the room. He paused beside Fargo. "Sorry about Sis. She's gone off the deep end, I'm afraid. Good luck on the drive," he said, the sudden burst of warmth unexpected.

"Thanks," Fargo said. "I'll be around a few days."

Owen Fargo walked on, drawing the swagger around him, a cloak, all surface bragging, Fargo mused. Abram Farrow brought his attention back as he pushed himself from the chair with an effort.

"You'll excuse me, Fargo. Ever since the accident I tire early," the man said.

"I'll be right back," Alberta said as she walked from the room with her husband. Fargo finished his coffee as he waited; he was at the window, looking out across the steer-packed corral under the moon when she returned. "You'll stay the night with us, I hope. We've three guest rooms," Alberta offered.

"Obliged. Never turn down a good offer," he answered, and she cast a little smile with her sidelong glance.

"I expect you don't," she remarked, and led the way to the end of the hall, where she opened the door and put on the lamp. He saw a neat room with a high-legged bed and a washstand and basin on a dresser. "I'm across the hall," she said. "If you need anything."

He met her lavender eyes. "Should I need anything?" he asked slowly.

"Not tonight," she said, and he watched the veil lower over the lavender rosemary eyes. She closed the door for him and he smiled as he turned to the bed, undressed,

41

and stretched out. He'd been right, he reflected. Let her make the first move. She would, when she was ready, he was convinced. Alberta Farrow was a simmering woman, the fire barely contained in the lavender eyes. He let the evening turn in his thoughts, a parade of surprise after surprise. Alberta Farrow clung, a promise wrapped in a puzzle.

She ran the Farrow ranch, Abram Farrow only a shell of a man. A shell in every way, he was sure. Alberta had substituted power for a husband. But it was not as simple as that, Fargo reflected. She was careful to let Abram think he still ran the Farrow ranch. Not as a gesture of kindness, Fargo grunted. It meant that her power was all on the surface yet. She still had to be careful. Money, titles, deeds, everything of real substance was plainly still in Abram Farrow's hands.

The family itself was a prairie storm of whirling tensions. Owen Farrow, a weak, self-indulgent sponge; Abram, a man trying to let what he had built sustain him; Alberta, a strong-willed woman with ambitions to dominate the ranch. And there was Janet, the wild and thoroughly bitchy Janet. The others had implied she wasn't playing with a full deck, but he didn't get those signals from her. All he got from Janet Farrow was hot-tempered bitchiness. She hadn't even considered apologizing to him. Being sorry never entered her mind and Fargo felt the anger stir inside him at once. He still had a score to settle with her and he let vague, idle thoughts pass through his mind until he rolled on his side, turned off his musings, and enjoyed the luxury of the good, soft bed.

He slept quickly and soundly.

3

Fargo let the Ovaro pause to nibble on the rich buffalo grass and scanned the low hills, his lake-blue eyes narrowed. He'd risen early and rode north in the cool, autumn sun. Janet Farrow had her own place, they'd said. It couldn't be all that far away, he'd reasoned, not with her riding over for dinner. He had sent the Ovaro up into the gentle hills that rose before the high plains country and paralleled a stand of red cedar that topped a low hill when he came to a sudden halt. He spied the horse, at the far side of the line of red cedars, tethered loosely to a low branch, a roan mare, a very particular, unmistakable roan mare.

Fargo rode forward, staying just below the red cedars until he was halfway past the stand. He turned, moved into the trees, and cut back through the wooded stretch, threading his way slowly until the roan mare came into view again, this time directly ahead of him. He picked up the sound of the water, then, and followed his ears through the trees until he came in sight of the small river that flowed slowly past the other edge of the cedars, undoubtedly one of the tributaries of the Big Sioux. He edged the horse forward toward the end of the treeline and saw the short brown hair bobbing in the water. He halted, still inside the trees, and his eyes swept the shoreline. The neat little mound of clothes lay just to his right at the edge of the shore atop a flat stone. Janet Farrow stayed mostly submerged in the water, and he caught a glimpse of nicely rounded shoulders, the soft swell of high breasts.

He moved into the clear and saw him at once as he walked the Ovaro to the bank of the small river. "Well, now, this is more than I expected. Must be my lucky day," he remarked.

She let only her head show above water as she glared at him. "What are you doing here?" She frowned.

"Came looking for you," Fargo said affably.

"You get out of here," Janet demanded.

"I thought you'd like another chance to say you're sorry for being so goddamn bitchy the other day," Fargo said.

"You could've helped me. I'm not sorry about anything and I'm not taking back anything," she snapped.

Fargo shrugged his broad shoulders almost sadly. "Then I'm paying back," he said as he leaned from the saddle and scooped her clothes up with one hand.

"You put those down," Janet Farrow shouted, started to rise out of the water, and sank back down immediately. Fargo started to turn the Ovaro in a tight circle. "You come back here. You can't leave me like this," Janet flung at him. He continued to turn his horse and heard the note of panic mix in with the fury in her voice. "Wait, you can't do this. Anything could happen to me like this," she called.

Fargo halted, speared her with a blue-steel stare. "That didn't bother you any the other day," he tossed back.

"It's not the same, damn you," she returned.

"You're right. The other day was worse. It was damn near night. I could've frozen," he said. "All you have to do is ride your naked little tail home. I'm being good to you."

"No, I couldn't ride back this way. And it's not that close," she protested. "What if I meet somebody?"

"Tell them you're trying out a new outfit . . . bare-skin." He chuckled and started the Ovaro forward.

"Bastard!" she shouted after him. "Coward and bastard." He didn't look back. She was one stubborn, rotten-tempered little package, as stubborn as she was pretty. He was letting her off easy. She'd get nothing more than embarrassment and maybe a sunburned butt. But he was satisfied. It'd maybe teach her a lesson to rein in that temper of hers. Maybe.

He headed the Ovaro along the edge of the red cedars. The high plateau stretched out to his left and the long line of trees to his right. He'd ridden but a few minutes, his eyes searching the ground as a matter of habit, when he reined the Ovaro to a halt.

He cursed softly as he saw the hoofprints that crossed in front of him and headed into the cedars, short-strided and unshod, the unmistakable prints of Indian ponies. Four, he counted, only minutes old, the tramped-down grass still moist. He steered the Ovaro into the woods and followed the line of hoofprints, quickly saw that the horsemen were moving south slowly, toward where Janet was probably still in the river.

"Damn," he whispered. He spurred the Ovaro forward, his eyes staying on the tracks for a few moments, then peering ahead through the cedars. They were riding Indian-file, he noted, and he swung in directly behind the trail. He followed a few minutes more and halted at the spot where the tracks moved apart. Dim in the filtered sun of the cedar woods, he spotted one of the Indians. He swept the woods and found the other three moving slowly. He squinted, strained his eyes at the nearest one. Sioux, he noted. They halted, lingered, letting their ponies chew on a large patch of red-leafed paintbrush. They were riding casually, but even so they'd be at the river in another few minutes.

He cursed again, swung the Ovaro around, and headed out of the cedars. He couldn't leave Janet to the Sioux, not naked as a jaybird, an invitation the Indian couldn't and wouldn't resist. He emerged from the trees and sent the Ovaro into a fast canter on the flatland alongside the stand of trees. He reached the river and darted into the trees again, to come out on the other side. Janet was half on shore and slid back into the water as she saw him. "Get out of there," he said. "Four Sioux will be here in a minute."

"Give me my clothes," she said.

He tossed the clothes at the edge of the bank. "You haven't time to dress. Take them and mount up," he told her.

"Turn around," she said.

"Honey, I'm not getting a Sioux arrow up my ass just because you want to be Miss Modest," Fargo said. "Get out of there and hit the saddle."

"Turn around," she said stubbornly. "Maybe you're making this up just so's you can enjoy yourself looking."

"Jesus, you're a stubborn package," he growled as he

turned away and peered into the red cedars. He caught the sudden sound of underbrush being pressed down hard. They were coming fast. They'd seen, smelled, or sensed something. "Ride, dammit," he said as he glanced over his shoulder. She had climbed onto the roan mare, her skirt tied around her waist and belly. He glimpsed nicely curved legs with round knees and her wet breasts pushed against the shirt she'd slipped on to outline the round, high mounds. He sent the Ovaro into a full gallop just as the Sioux appeared in the cedars, and he headed the horse down the riverbank where the ground was firm underfoot. Flinging a glance behind, he saw Janet stay close. The Sioux had lost precious seconds emerging from the cedars, but he saw them spur their ponies on as Janet drew alongside him. She pointed to a pair of sandstone high-pinnacled rocks that jutted up at the edge of the flatland.

"We could hold them off there," she shouted.

"We've a good start. Keep running," he said, bent low in the saddle, and urged the Ovaro on. Janet stayed close, the roan mare a good, fast horse, he saw. The skirt tied around her flapped in the wind and he saw one lovely thigh and the soft fold of her skin where it met the saddle. He threw another glance backward and saw the Sioux in pursuit but falling back, their short-legged ponies unable to hang in stride for stride.

But the Sioux wouldn't break off a chase for that reason alone. They knew a quarry could make a wrong move, a horse could stumble or run out of steam. They persisted, and Fargo kept the Ovaro racing even as the Indians continued to lose ground. Finally, he saw the Sioux wheel away, slow, and head north toward the high plains. He slowed and finally drew to a halt, dismounted as the Ovaro pawed the ground and noisily blew air.

Janet halted and saw him take in her legs, the round curve of her rear where the tied-on skirt had pushed upward.

"No reason you can't turn around now," she muttered.

He drew a deep sigh and turned from her. "Hurry up. I might change my mind," he said, and he heard her slip from the roan and draw on clothes. When he turned, she came out from the other side of the horse, skirt and shirt in place, but her breasts still made wet, clinging mounds in the shirt.

"I'll thank you for coming back to warn me, but nothing else," she said with a defensive glare.

"Don't strain yourself," Fargo remarked, and saw her lips tighten.

"Some men would've taken to the rocks to bring down a few Sioux," she said. "You ran."

He shrugged. She was determined to convince herself he was a coward. It was easier than admitting she'd been all wrong the other afternoon, and he decided to play the role awhile longer. "Never fight Indians unless I have to," he said. "They're full of surprises."

Janet Farrow made a skeptical sound as she climbed back on the roan. He mounted the Ovaro and saw her watching him with a small, quizzical frown. "You're a strange one. All you wanted to do was run. Yet you came back to warn me. Why?" she asked. "Conscience?"

"Guess so," he answered uncertainly.

"I suppose I ought to be glad you've got a conscience," she said.

"I could use some coffee," Fargo said.

"Nerves acting up?" she asked, and couldn't keep the disdain out of her voice.

" 'Fraid so," he said, holding to his role.

"Alberta will be happy to get some for you," Janet snapped.

He let himself seem injured. "What's that mean?" he asked.

"I saw the way she looked at you," Janet answered.

Fargo swore silently. For all her fury at the house she had been quick to pick up on things. Female intuition, he figured. It never ceased to amaze him.

"You've got that all wrong," he said.

"Hah!" Janet snorted derisively.

"You don't get along with her, do you? Or the rest of the family, either?" Fargo remarked.

"Their fault," Janet snapped, her pert face setting itself firmly.

"All their fault?" he questioned.

"All," she repeated with unyielding firmness.

"You don't give any, do you?" he said.

"No need to when you're right," she returned.

"Who was this Jeff fellow you mentioned?" Fargo asked casually.

The green-flecked hazel eyes narrowed at him. "You're asking a lot of questions," she said, and he half-shrugged. "A man who worked for me," she told him.

"How'd he get killed?" Fargo asked.

She fastened an annoyed glance on him. "Look, I'm not going to waste time going into it with the likes of you. Go get your coffee from Alberta," she said and wheeled her horse in a half-circle. "God, I don't know how you got a reputation as a trailsman." She put the roan into a fast canter and he watched her go along the edge of the high plains and turn south, dip downward, and vanish from sight.

He smiled to himself as he rode the Ovaro at a walk, following her tracks. Maybe the rest of the family was right about her: she was certainly defensive and full of nettles. He followed her trail down into the low flatland, past a heavy thicket of elms. She had stayed close to the trees and he rode over the top of a low rise and saw the house, modest corrals spreading out from one side.

He reined to a halt and espied the roan mare, unsaddled, in one of the corrals, and he edged under the widespread, open branches of an elm. The house, log and frame combination, had none of the substance of the Farrow ranch, but it was neat, well-tended, and wore a fresh coat of paint. A woodshed ran along one side and a small, attached hut bordered the other. As he surveyed the spread, a man emerged from the attached hut, thin and stooped, an old and battered stetson on his head. He pushed a wheelbarrow of kindling wood, and he paused, lifted his hat to brush a kerchief over his forehead. It was too far to see clearly, but Fargo made out white hair, a weathered face. The man was in his sixties, maybe seventy, Fargo guessed as he watched him resume pushing the wheelbarrow to the woodshed.

The man returned to the hut as Fargo stayed motionless under the elm. Janet emerged from the house after a while for a brief trip to the well with a bucket, and disappeared back inside. Fargo moved the horse along the elms and saw a small stable at the back of the house. He turned the Ovaro and headed back through the trees, came out onto the open flatland, and made for the Farrow ranch.

As he rode, he thought about the hidden currents running between Janet and the rest of the Farrows. He wanted to be sure that whatever they were wouldn't spill over onto the drive. It was no idle concern. Family feuds had a way of involving everybody on hand and he wondered what might explode around him. He decided to probe further, starting with Alberta.

Pushing the Ovaro into a trot, he pulled his jacket shut as a cold blast of air whipped at him suddenly. He watched the clouds sweeping the high sky. Winter was sending out its messages for those who knew how to listen. He saw a flight of black-and-gray Canada geese flying low on their way south, the sight always a strangely lonely one. His eyes swept the sky again. He'd be breaking trail southward. That'd give them another thirty days on the good side of the first real cold weather, and he was grateful for that. Abram Farrow had stretched time to the limit in waiting this long to drive the herd.

Fargo kept the Ovaro at a steady trot until he reached the ranch. He saw a half-dozen hands bringing in another line of steers from the far grazing pasture, Seth Bailey's ruddy face at the head of the procession. The Trailsman dismounted at the main house and saw Alberta appear in the doorway, a long, deep-blue dress clinging to her tall figure, touching the tips of her long breasts with fleeting provocativeness. As he walked to the doorway he caught the irritation in the set of her lips. "I thought you'd be around this morning," she said.

"Been riding, checking the countryside," he said calmly.

The irritation stayed in her face. "I had Yakes take Abram to Bill Stattner in Owensboro to buy winter feed. Abram likes to do that himself," Alberta said. "But they're due back now. You've been gone all morning."

"Sorry," Fargo said. "I miss out on something?" he added innocently, and saw the thin veil slide over Alberta's eyes, the lavender becoming a smoky blue.

"Possibly," she said.

"Maybe I'll get another chance," Fargo said blandly.

"Maybe," she echoed, and he saw the satisfaction glint in her eyes. She was still in charge, still the one to make the first move. He'd done nothing to destroy the game so far.

"I could stand some coffee," he said.

"The pot's always on," Alberta said, and led him into the large kitchen, where a white enameled coffeepot bubbled atop a low flame over the cooking hearth. She poured a mug of coffee for him and one for herself. He chose sentences carefully, leaned back against one wall.

"Ran into Janet," he said idly. "She's sure got a burr under her saddle," he remarked.

"What happened?" Alberta asked too quickly.

"Happened to mention that hand who was killed. She damn near bit my head off when I asked about him," Fargo said.

"Naturally," Alberta said with disdain. "She's turned the whole thing around just to get sympathy. Jeff Halder got into a gunfight and got himself killed for it. It's as simple as that, but she's been saying he was killed because he worked for her."

"Why would he be killed because of that?" Fargo asked.

"No reason I can think of," Alberta said.

"Doesn't make much sense, does it?" Fargo said as he tried to coax more from Alberta, but he saw her set her face with cold righteousness.

"None at all. We told you, she thinks people are plotting against her. She's really a little sick," Alberta said.

"Seems so," Fargo agreed. Right or wrong, Alberta was standing on that explanation for Janet, and he'd decided not to press further when he saw the figure appear in the doorway. Yakes filled the entranceway, his sullen face glowering as he looked at Fargo and back at Alberta.

"You're back," the woman said smoothly.

"Mr. Abram wants you to help record the feed bags while we store them," Yakes said, made the request almost an order. "He's waiting in the barn," the foreman said.

"All right, I'll get the ledger book," Alberta said. She tossed a half-apologetic glance at Fargo and strode from the kitchen.

Fargo took a sip of his coffee and felt the foreman's eyes on him. "She won't be coming back. This'll take the rest of the day," Yakes growled. More than a passing remark, Fargo noted silently, words tinged with a warning.

"Thanks," Fargo said, drained the last of the coffee, and sauntered out of the house as Yakes followed. The foreman's sullenness was more than protective. He had obvious ambitions to be something more than foreman, and Fargo thought of Alberta's comment that Yakes was a man who didn't understand his own limitations. Was that it? Fargo wondered. Or had she contributed, toyed with him to transfer his loyalties from Abram to herself? It was easy to imagine her doing that.

Fargo paused outside and watched Yakes propel his heavy-shouldered form to the barn. When the man disappeared inside, he found a bucket and decided to give the Ovaro a proper wash and curry. The task used up the rest of the afternoon, but he enjoyed the satisfaction that was his when the magnificent steed glistened and gleamed. The dusk shadows had already stretched across the corrals when Alberta came from the barn, Abram on her arm and Yakes drawing up behind. She flashed a quick glance at Fargo as she took Abram into the house. Yakes went on to the bunkhouse. Fargo began to saddle the Ovaro and had just fastened the rear jockey to the saddle skirt when Alberta reappeared. She hurried over to him.

"Abram wants to go over the books tonight," she said, and he heard the irritation in her voice. "Sometimes he gets these bursts of energy. He'll be absolutely useless for days afterward, but when he's this way, I have to work with him."

"Why not?" Fargo said blandly.

Her eyes narrowed. "I had other plans," she said.

He smiled. "There's tomorrow. But you're running out of time, I'd guess," he said.

The lavender eyes stayed narrowed. "What do you mean?" she asked.

He let his smile widen. She still wanted to play games. "I mean whatever you mean," he said. "You're the boss lady."

"Indeed," Alberta murmured. "You'll use the guest room tonight?"

"Can't say for sure. Might want to stay in the field and do some real early scouting," he answered. "I'll be back later in the morning, in any case."

She nodded and turned away, plainly dissatisfied with his answer and everything else.

The night descended quickly. Fargo finished saddling the horse and, reins in hand, walked to the entrance to the ranch. Seth Bailey nodded to him as he carried a saddle to the stable. Once past the corrals, Fargo swung onto the Ovaro and rode out onto the flatland. He turned northwest and let the fast-rising moon outline the slow, gentle hills that led to the high plains. He headed toward Janet Farrow's place, plans not really formed, but he was convinced he wanted another try at

54

drawing the hot-tempered little package out. He'd listened to Alberta's answers on Janet, all of them logical enough, yet he sensed that something important was being sidestepped. Alberta's explanations made sense and yet they didn't. Little things didn't quite add up, or perhaps he just needed another, longer, more critical look at Janet Farrow. He rode unhurriedly and came into sight of the thicket of elms. He approached from the down side of the trees, stayed along the lower edge, and had just started up the slow rise of land when he glimpsed the three riders in the trees at the other side.

He halted, edged the Ovaro forward another few yards. The men, all in dark clothes and dark hats, sat on their horses along the treeline at the far side of the thicket. Fargo let himself continue to ride forward and knew the three men had spotted him as he moved past the trees. He continued to ride forward slowly, giving no sign that he had seen them. He'd almost reached the top of the low hill when the horse and rider came over the top from the other side, the moonlight touching a white shirt and, above it, short hair and a pert face. Janet halted as he came up to her.

"What are you doing here?" She frowned.

"Was going to pay you a visit," Fargo said.

"I'm on my way to Rock Hollow," she said.

"I'll ride along," he said.

She paused, shrugged. "Suit yourself," she answered as she moved the roan forward. He pulled the Ovaro alongside her and, without moving his head, flicked a glance along the far edge of the thicket of elms. The three riders were still there. They'd drawn back deeper into the trees and he caught the outline of one hat only because he could pinpoint his glance.

"Get your coffee this morning?" Janet asked with a touch of disdain.

"I did. Coffee and answers, more than I got from you," he told her.

"What kind of answers?" she asked.

He rode slowly and she pulled back with him. "About that hand of yours that was shot. Seems he was killed in a gunfight," Fargo remarked.

Janet's pert face turned pugnacious at once. "Alberta told you that," she snapped, and he nodded. "It's not so. He was gunned down deliberately. There was no gunfight," she said.

Fargo let his lips purse in thought as he flicked another glance at the thicket of elms above where they rode. He picked up the outline of two of the riders as the moonlight filtered through the trees. "Not how I heard it," Fargo commented.

"Well, you heard wrong. Fact is, I'm going to meet a man at the Silver Garter with information for me about who hired Jeff's killers," Janet said.

Fargo let his brows lift. "How'd you find him?" he asked.

"He found me," Janet said. "Came up to me a few days ago when I was shopping in town, said he needed money enough to stake a claim up in Oregon and he'd sell me what I wanted to know for the money. We agreed to meet at the Silver Garter tonight, just outside."

"You get his name?" Fargo inquired.

"Chuck Conway," Janet said, and Fargo glanced up as the trees came to an end and Janet continued on over the gently rolling flatland. He glanced back and barely glimpsed the three men leave the tree cover. They were hanging far back but they continued to tail them and he brought the Ovaro up beside Janet as she increased speed.

"Why would your hand be gunned down because he worked for you?" he asked.

"A warning. Scare me off," she said.

"Scare you off what?" he persisted.

She cast a long, speculative look at him. "You saying you believe me?" she asked.

"Not saying yes or no yet," he answered.

"Then you can wait till I meet with Chuck Conway for anything more," she snapped, her temper flaring.

"Damn, you've got a short fuse, honey," Fargo said as they came in sight of Rock Hollow.

"I'd like being believed for a change," Janet said tightly.

Fargo cast a quick glance behind and saw a low rock formation to the right and the distant, barely visible shapes of the three riders heading for it. He made a mental note of the spot and headed into town beside Janet, tossed a quick glance at her pert, pretty face. She was plainly unaware that the three men had been waiting outside her place and had followed them to the edge of town. Nothing made a hell of a lot of sense yet and he pushed speculation away as he rode down the dark of Main Street with her.

When they reached the Silver Garter, the still of the town shattered with the noise and the light that streamed from the dance hall. Janet halted beside the hitching post and Fargo watched her scan the shadows edging the double doors of the saloon. Two drunks pushed the doors open, to stagger out into the street and weave away. A dance-hall girl in a low-cut black dress came outside for a brief moment, drew in deep breaths of air, and then returned inside. "He's not here," Janet said, glanced at Fargo, and caught the brief thought that had flashed through his mind. "I didn't make it up. There was a Chuck Conway and he was going to meet me here," she flared instantly.

"Maybe he's inside having a drink," Fargo said as he swung to the ground. Janet, her round face filled with concern, walked into the saloon with him. The noise and bright light from a huge crystal chandelier was almost a physical blow. He swept the inside of the Silver Garter with a quick glance, dance-hall girls and their customers crowding the small open floor space, tables beyond in a semicircle, and a long, oak bar taking up most of one wall. Beyond the bar he saw the curtain screening off the room for the serious gamblers, marked by a big playing card hung on the curtain. His gaze paused at the little, fashion-plate figure of Ed Carver at one end of the bar. The little man stood upon a platform that let him see the entire room, and his gold stickpin gleamed under the lights.

"I don't see him. He's not here," Janet murmured.

Fargo's eyes were still on the dapper little figure as Ed Carver stepped from the platform and deftly made his way through the crowd toward them. The man halted before Janet, his ceaselessly darting eyes surveying her with curiosity.

"Miss Farrow, I believe," he said.

"Yes, Mr. Carver," Janet said, her eyes going over the little man's head as she swept the room again with a frown.

"Can I help you?" he asked, flicking a glance at the big man beside her.

"I was to meet someone here, outside," Janet said.

Ed Carver's tight face managed an expression of mild surprise. "Hope his name wasn't Conway," he said, and

Fargo saw Janet's lips part as apprehension flooded her face.

"Why?" she asked.

"A fool named Conway got into a gunfight and was killed a half-hour ago," the little man said casually. "Just one of those things."

"No," Janet snapped.

Carver frowned. "How's that?" he asked.

"Not just one of those things," Janet said through tight lips. "Too neat. Too damn convenient. Who did it? Who killed him?"

The little saloonkeeper nodded to the bar and a man in a dark-green shirt nursing a shot glass of whiskey. "Billy Drain. Your friend made the mistake of tangling with Billy," he said.

Janet strode toward the bar, her fists clenched, and Fargo saw the man turn as she reached him. Billy Drain stared at the girl with small, round eyes hard as stones out of a thin face that wore a perpetual sneer. But it was the gun in his holster that caught Fargo's eye, an ivory-plated grip on a Colt Frontier, the holster hung slightly forward of his hip, thin rawhide thongs tying it to his leg. A gunfighter's outfit.

"Who paid you to do it?" Janet flung at the man.

Billy Drain's stone eyes stared at her. "What the hell are you talking about, sister?" he growled.

"Conway. Who paid you to kill him?" Janet said.

Fargo saw the stone eyes narrow a fraction. "Nobody. He had a big mouth. I closed it—permanent," the man said.

"You were paid to pick a fight with him, to make sure he wouldn't talk to me," Janet said.

"You're crazy, sister," the gunfighter said.

"And you're a damn liar," Janet snapped.

"Watch your mouth, doll," Billy Drain snarled, and Fargo saw his little round eyes grow smaller. Others were watching. Billy Drain couldn't let a girl bully him. "You got two seconds to get your ass out of here," he rasped.

"You going to kill me, too?" Janet returned.

Fargo saw the man flick a glance at those looking on, and his eyes returned to Janet. "Won't bother me any," the man said, and Fargo knew the answer was no empty threat. "But first I'll shut your mouth. You need some lessons," Drain said, and took a step forward.

"No need for that. She's leaving," Fargo said.

Billy Drain didn't glance at him as he moved toward Janet. "Fuck off, mister. No little bitch is going to call me a liar and get away with it," the gunfighter said.

"Forget it," Fargo said, and stepped forward.

Billy Drain turned his eyes on the big man for the first time. "You lookin' for a pine box, mister?" he said thinly.

"Just leave the girl be," Fargo said softly.

"Fargo, stay out of it," Janet said. "He'll gun you down the way he did Conway. I'll take care of myself."

Fargo heard the concern in her voice, but it was too late. Billy Drain enjoyed killing and he was certain he had an easy mark. He wouldn't be turned off now and his words were a confirmation.

"You're a dead man, mister," the gunfighter said, an edge of icy satisfaction in his voice. The room grew still and Fargo saw those nearest backing away, pushing to the side. Billy Drain took a step back, turned to face him. The man expected fear from those he faced, the fear that always gave him that split-second advantage. Fargo smiled, inwardly. Surprise would turn the tables on the man, force him into fatal mistakes.

"You are ugly and you are a stupid shit tinhorn

gunfighter," Fargo said, and saw Billy Drain's stone eyes fill with astonishment and rage.

"Son of a bitch," the man rasped as he went for his gun. But rage destroyed the smoothness of his draw. His hand slapped at the grip, slowing his draw a precious fraction of a second. The big Colt .45 seemed to fly into Fargo's hand and fire, two shots that blew apart Billy Drain's stomach. The gunfighter staggered backward, astonishment still holding his face as his midsection spilled from him in a thick red torrent. Fargo had holstered his gun before Billy Drain collapsed on the floor, half bent over, as though he were resting instead of dead. Fargo saw the little saloonkeeper studying him with a thoughtful expression.

"Very impressive, mister," Ed Carver commented.

"The girl and I were right about him," the big man said, and turned to see Janet staring at him, her lips parted, amazement in the hazel eyes. "Let's get out of here," he muttered, and took her by the elbow.

"I want to talk to you," Janet said, finding her voice.

"Later," he growled, and saw a half-dozen men had stepped from the gambling room and watched from in front of the curtain. He propelled Janet out of the saloon and released his grip on her arm. "Ride," he said, swung onto the Ovaro, and went into a fast trot. He rode from Rock Hollow, across the flatland, and Janet caught up to him.

"Can we talk now?" she asked.

"No," he snapped as he rode past the rock formation, continued on, and it was only when he neared the line of elms that he glanced backward. The high moon just caught the outline of the three riders that followed after them once again. His lips pulled into a tight line, he steered the Ovaro into the elms and Janet pushed her horse alongside him.

"Why through here? We'd make better time outside," she said.

Fargo slowed the Ovaro almost to a walk and she fell back with him. "We've got company. They've been following us since we left your place," he said, and saw her brows lift in surprise. "Just keep moving along and don't look back," he said as she started to turn in the saddle.

She obeyed and her voice was low. "They close behind us?" she asked.

"They'll be coming along soon. They'll be listening for two horses and that's what they're going to hear," Fargo said, and handed Janet the Ovaro's reins. "Take it slow," he added. He pushed himself back over the horse's rump and landed silent as a cat on the balls of his feet.

He moved noiselessly across the ground thick with fallen elm leaves and slid behind a clump of tall brush. Colt in hand, he waited for the dark shapes of the three horsemen to appear through the trees. Only a glimmer of moonlight filtered down and the three riders passed a scant six feet from where he crouched, two riding abreast of each other, the third behind.

He waited till the last one had gone by before he rose. "Hold it right there," he called out, and saw the three men turn in their saddles as they reined up. "Throw your guns down nice and slow, and nobody gets hurt," Fargo ordered. He saw the last rider nearest him begin to slowly move one hand toward his holster, reach the gun butt with two fingers. He had started to lift the gun when the other two drove spurs into their horses as they yanked at their guns. Fargo swung the Colt and fired, and one of the men flew from his horse with a groan of pain. But the other two seized the moment and dived from their horses. Fargo heard them land in the brush and he threw himself flat as they emptied their guns at him in a furious volley of shots.

He lay flattened to the ground as he heard the branches breaking just over his head as the fusillade of shots tore through the brush. The furious gunfire stopped as suddenly as it had begun. They were hurrying to reload, Fargo knew, and he pushed himself up, peered through the near-total darkness. A dark bulk moved and Fargo's big Colt barked twice. The dark bulk became a figure that toppled forward through the brush to land half across a fallen piece of log. Fargo threw himself flat again, but the last man held his fire and Fargo lay motionless. After a few moments he heard the rustling of brush. The man was crawling, likely toward his horse. But he'd be watching as he crawled, waiting for a target to rise.

Fargo stayed flattened and let his ears trace the man's progress. He'd wait till the man reached his horse, and he'd known that moment by the change in the sound of the brush being pushed aside. His quarry would have to come up into the open then, long enough to make him a target. Fargo stayed motionless, hardly breathing as he listened to the brush being pressed down.

Suddenly the soft sound was drowned out by the thud of approaching hoofbeats. "Goddamn," Fargo muttered as he strained his ears, but he could hear only the hoofbeats. He half-rose, peered through the trees, and saw Janet riding up, holding the Ovaro alongside her. He caught the flash of movement to his left and saw the man hunched over in the saddle of his horse, hardly more than a small black shadow as the horse started to run. Fargo brought up the Colt and fired as the man half-rose in the saddle to turn his horse between two thick trees. He saw the dark shadow rise, arms flung outward, and topple sideways from the horse. "Damn," he swore again. He'd wanted the time to aim carefully enough to only wing him so he could answer questions, but the figure lay crumpled and still. Janet reined to a halt and he glared at her. "Why'd you rush back, dammit?" he barked.

"Heard the shooting and then it stopped. I came back to see if you were hurt," she said.

"Thanks," he said unhappily as his eyes swept the fallen figures. "Whatever they figured to do, they won't be doing it," he said, and glanced at Janet. "Not bad for a coward and a fraud, eh?" he commented.

"Why'd you let me think that?" she asked.

"Let you? Honey, that was all your idea. You must be part jackrabbit the way you jump to conclusions."

He saw her eyes narrow. "You let me go on believing it. You played the part. You even needed coffee to quiet your nerves after the Sioux chased us," she said.

"I didn't want to ruin my image," he said. "You were so sure about everything."

She managed to draw a touch of contriteness into her face. "Maybe I was a little unreasonable at the pond," she murmured.

"Unreasonable?" He frowned. "That sure as hell is the wrong word. Saying you've been out of line comes hard to you, doesn't it?"

A low groan cut off her answer and he spun on his heel. The man that had fallen across the log groaned again, and Fargo was beside him in three long-legged strides. He knelt down and saw the man's eyelids flutter open. "Talk, man. You've nothing to lose by it now," he said, and the man's eyes managed to stay open. "Why'd you watch her? Why'd you tail us?" Fargo asked.

The man coughed and words fell from his lips along

with a trickle of blood that coursed down the side of his chin. "Make . . . make sure . . ." he rasped, a whispered sound almost drowned out by the hard rattle of his breath.

"Go on," Fargo urged. "Make sure what?"

The man's eyelids flickered, closed, opened again. "She didn't . . . didn't . . ." the man said, and suddenly the silence seemed loud. The hard rattle of his breath was gone, his eyes closed. His last gasped moments were over and Fargo rose to his feet. He speared Janet with a sharp stare.

"They wanted to make sure you didn't do or see or say something. I want to know what the hell this is all about, dammit. No more holding back," he demanded.

"All right, I'll show you what it's all about," she said with a burst of anger, and whirled, pulled herself onto the roan, and raced away. He swung onto his horse and followed her as she veered out of the elms and onto the flat, open land, riding hard. Fargo was content to stay behind her since she seemed to be riding straight for her place. Alberta and the others had said she imagined things and twisted truth to get sympathy for herself. He couldn't dismiss the accusations entirely yet, but she hadn't imagined Chuck Conway or the three men who'd followed her. Maybe she hadn't imagined anything else, either. Maybe they were misjudging Janet, he pondered as he followed the roan over the low rise and saw the neat house come into sight.

Janet slowed, reined to a halt in front of her house, and Fargo saw the door open as he rode up. The old man came out, his white hair catching the light from the room behind, a big old plains rifle in his hands. "It's me, Bixby," Janet called out, and dismounted. Fargo swung down to the ground. The old man surveyed him with blue eyes that wore both weariness and wisdom. "Skye Fargo . . . Bixby Bunker," Janet introduced. "Bixby's my right hand."

"Kind of an old right hand," Bixby Bunker said as Janet walked to the small table behind the house. She pushed the door open, turned up a lamp hanging on one wall, and Fargo followed her in to where a calf looked up from a square stall. "There . . . that's what it's all about," Janet bit out.

Fargo took in the calf with an experienced eye. It was unlike any calf he'd ever seen before, a light-gray-white in color with no markings, a big calf with hips more square and pronounced than he'd ever seen. He squatted down and the calf ambled over to nuzzle him with a strong, square snout.

Fargo looked up at Janet. "Talk," he said. "What and why?"

"That is a Charolais calf," Janet said, and the questions were in the frown he tossed at her. "A French breed. I'd sent for two, but one died on the way."

"You'd better start at the beginning," Fargo said, and stood up as the calf went over to a feedbox.

"Over coffee," she said, and led the way into the house through a connecting door that opened onto the kitchen. Bixby Bunker had a coffeepot bubbling, and he set out two mugs, handing one to Fargo. Janet perched on the edge of a heavy wood chair and Bixby Bunker poured the coffee and left the neat kitchen with a nod at Fargo. Janet's eyes surveyed Fargo with a sober stare and he saw her groping to choose words. "I have an idea. It's not popular with some people," she began.

"That calf is part of it?" Fargo said.

"That calf is it," Janet answered. "Nothing is being bred around here but longhorns and whiteface. The long and terrible winters are too hard on both breeds, especially the longhorns, and the hot summers bring plagues that take a heavy toll of the whiteface."

"But they're still being stocked and sold," Fargo said.

"With too many losses. I say we need a hardier and meatier steer to raise and maybe crossbreed," Janet said.

"The Charolais?"

"Yes. They're used to the snows of the French Alps and they give more beef per pound than longhorns or whiteface. It'll take some time to start a good herd, but I know they could work out," she told him.

"What's all this to do with killing and fighting?" Fargo questioned.

"Somebody's afraid I'll bring in a new and better breed and put them out of business," she said.

"Such as?"

"Barnaby Tilden," Janet snapped at once. "Know him?"

"Heard the name," Fargo said.

"He breeds and raises young stock, some hogs, too, sells them to ranchers all over this part of Iowa," she said, and Fargo recalled how Alice Calkin had told him much the same thing about Barnaby Tilden. "He has everything invested in whiteface and longhorns and he doesn't want a new and better breed coming in. If I came up with a breed cattle buyers welcomed and was easier for ranchers to keep healthy, he'd be out of business. That's why Jeff was killed, to warn me, scare me off. But I don't scare easily."

"Barnaby Tilden the only one you can think of?" Fargo asked.

"Could be one of the smaller breeders, but I don't think so," she answered.

"Why not?"

"He's got the money to hire paid killers, he's close enough to know what I'm trying to do, and he has the most to lose. He doesn't want to see a hardier breed here. The more steers ranchers lose every freezing winter and tick-filled summer, the more new stock he can sell them."

Fargo pondered her words. Her logic made sense, yet he'd learned long ago that logic and truth weren't always one and the same. "Your family doesn't seem too happy about you," he remarked.

"They're upset with me, I know that," Janet said. "But it's nothing more than that. Barnaby Tilden's the one."

Fargo half-shrugged. "Things aren't always what they seem," he told her, and let a sly smile touch his lips. "But then you found that out tonight. Don't forget it," he said.

Janet's round, pert face admitted a flash of sheepishness. "Being wrong about one thing doesn't mean I'm wrong about everything else," she said.

"Maybe not," he conceded as he finished the coffee and got to his feet.

"What happens with you now?" Janet asked.

"Be leaving soon. Maybe tomorrow. The last of the herd's in from pasture," he said.

She frowned as she turned thoughts in her mind. "Can you stop back before you leave?" she asked.

"Suppose I could," he said.

She walked with him as he moved to the door. "Thanks, again, for tonight," Janet said, her pert, pretty face very serious. "It'd been hard, knowing someone was killed on my account and wondering what'll happen next. I'm not always so . . . so . . ."

"Rotten-tempered?" he offered.

"So easily upset," she corrected firmly. "It was good, your being there tonight. I didn't feel so alone." The green-flecked hazel eyes looked up at him as she suddenly reached up and her lips were on his, a warm, softly firm surprise. She lingered just long enough for him to start to respond and then she pulled away. "Thank you, again, Fargo," she murmured.

"You're made of surprises," he remarked.

"Surprises and stubbornness," she said. "Sometimes you get one, sometimes the other, sometimes both."

"I like the surprise," Fargo said."Think you could arrange more of the same?"

She half-shrugged and her pert face stayed grave. "I don't know. Maybe," she said.

He reached out and his arm encircled her waist, softly firm, a little chunky, and he pulled her to him, pressed his mouth on hers a little less than gently. He pushed with his lips, let his tongue press against her, and felt her lips part, draw in the tip of his soft wetness for an instant. Her breath came, half-gasped, and he held her tight against him, the high, round breasts pressed into his chest. He let her go when he felt her palms start to press against his shoulders. "Just to help you make up your mind," he told her, and saw protest and the touch of desire in the hazel eyes that frowned back at him.

"I can make up my own mind without help," she said quickly, and he laughed as he opened the door and walked from the house. She closed it at once and he strode to the Ovaro, pausing as he saw the shock of white hair gleam in the moonlight, the figure of Bixby Bunker under it leaning against a fence post.

"You going to stay on to help her?" the old man asked.

Fargo shook his head. "Got to break trail for a cattle drive," he said.

"Too bad," Bixby Bunker grunted.

"She's got you," Fargo said.

"She'll need more than I can give her," the man said.

"Maybe she ought to put this idea of a new breed aside for a while," Fargo remarked.

Bixby Bunker's leathered face wrinkled still further. "Not her. She'll push on. Too stubborn. Always was, even as a little girl," he said.

"You've known her a long time," Fargo said.

"Used to work for her mother," Bixby Bunker said.

"You know Barnaby Tilden?" Fargo queried.

"I do," Bixby said. "You askin' if I agree with Janet about him?" Fargo smiled as he nodded at the old man's quickness. "Yes and no," Bixby said. "He's got the most to lose if a new breed put him out of business, but I never figured him for the kind of man who'd hire killers to do his work."

"I don't understand why a new, better breed would put so many people out of business. The Farrow ranch sells whiteface and longhorns. They could just stock the new breed if it turns out better."

"Time and money, that's why," Bixby answered. "They'd all stick with their stock for a few years. If Janet's Charolais really caught on with the cattle buyers, it'd take the others at least a couple of years to build up a herd. She'd be years ahead of them and have most of the market by then. They'd all be sucking hind tit while now they're in the catbird seat."

Fargo pulled himself onto his horse and turned to ride away. "I'll keep in touch till I leave, but that won't be long," he said to Bixby.

"Appreciate that," Bixby said, and Fargo sent the Ovaro into a trot and headed through the night toward the Farrow ranch. He found himself thinking about Barnaby Tilden as he wondered if he had sent the three riders out to watch Janet. Her words about the man clung, full of reason and logic. But he kept remembering what Alice Calkin had said about Barnaby Tilden for paying her to raise his overflow stock. "Barnaby is a good man who believes in doing the right thing," Alice had said. The picture she drew of the man didn't fit the one Janet gave.

Fargo let his thoughts continue to idle as he rode through the moon-touched night. There were others, Janet had admitted even as she dismissed them. Was that dismissal a mistake? Fargo wondered. Was she unwilling to look past Barnaby Tilden, especially at the antagonism of her own family. He understood that more, now, each of the Farrows with their own reason for painting Janet as a victim of her own imagination and desire for sympathy. Abram Farrow hadn't the strength any longer for starting anything new. He wanted things to stay as they were, smooth and untroubled. But he hadn't the strength to be more than unhappy about Janet, either, Fargo was certain. Alberta was a different kettle of fish. There was no love lost between her and Janet, and she was a strong-willed, determined woman. She wanted to inherit the Double-C ranch just the way it was, running smoothly and making money. Fargo's eyes narrowed for a moment in thought. He didn't see Alberta with enough hate to send out hired guns after Janet, he mused. But he couldn't write off the possibility. Which brought him to Owen Farrow. He wouldn't act out of strength, but out of fear and desperation. The thought of anything that could destroy his source of easy income would set him off. How far would he go? Fargo pondered. Far enough to hire guns against his own sister? That took the kind of ruthless strength that didn't seem part of Owen Farrow.

The questions were for Janet to unravel. Her problems had intruded enough and he'd be happy not to see them intrude further. He had a trail to break and that was job enough.

The darkened buildings of the Farrow ranch came into view and he slowed the horse to a walk and quietly moved past the bunkhouse and halted before the main house. He tied the horse to the hitching post, entered the house, and made his way down the dark hallway to the guest room on silent steps. He opened the door, closed it softly, and the lamplight came on low to cast a soft yellow glow in the room. Alberta sat on the edge of the bed, her hand still at the lamp, her black hair loose, hanging down over a long nightdress of deep blue buttoned at the neck.

"I've been waiting for you," she said with just a hint of reproof in her tone.

"Got involved," he said as he moved to stand before her.

Alberta's lavender eyes searched his, the hint of reproof echoed in their depths. "Involved in what?" she asked.

He paused, let thoughts turn inside his head, and decided to get her reactions. "Saving Janet's hide," he said, and saw surprise flicker in the lavender eyes. Omitting only that he had gone to Janet's place first, he recounted everything else that had happened in short, flat sentences, facts without color. He watched Alberta as he spoke, but saw that she kept her face expressionless until he finished, when her voice held just a trace of waspishness.

"I'd say Janet was very lucky you happened to be on hand," she said.

"I'd say so, too." He smiled affably. "She told me her ideas about bringing in a new breed."

"She ask advice?" Alberta said slowly.

"No, she just told me about her ideas. But one thing came out of it. You've all been wrong about her imagining things," he said mildly. "Those sidewinders tonight were real enough."

"Apparently we have been too hasty to assume things about Janet," Alberta agreed, letting her lips purse in thought. "But that doesn't change my opinion of what she's doing," Alberta added, her openness disarming.

"Seems a lot of folks feel the same about that," Fargo commented casually.

"Of course. She's going to upset the whole market," Alberta said. "If she succeeds, that is, which I doubt. But that has angered a lot of people."

"Somebody's angry enough to hire killers," Fargo remarked.

"I wouldn't know about that, but I do know Janet won't listen to reason. She wants to make a name for herself and she doesn't care who she'll hurt doing it. You'd best keep that in mind, Fargo," Alberta said.

"I will." He nodded.

"Enough of Janet. I didn't wait here to talk about her," Alberta said with annoyance. "I've other business."

"Business?" he echoed, his brows lifting as he let himself look disappointed.

A tiny smile edged her lips. "Business first, always," she said. "I've a problem and I decided you're the man for the job. There's a payroll to be picked up in Dodge City and I need it back here right away. I want you to bring it back."

"Why me? Yakes will be there," Fargo queried.

"The boys always get half a week off when they finish a drive. It's part of their employment contract. I can't and wouldn't change that, but I need that payroll. That means you'll have to turn around and start right back and ride hard. I'm willing to make it worth your while. Two hundred dollars' worth, Fargo."

Fargo's brows lifted again. "That's a lot of money when you could have it for free a week later," he commented.

"Yes, but a week is very important at this time. I need the cash to pay suppliers and you earn a nice, fat payday because of it," Alberta said.

He shrugged. "That's fine with me. I don't mind turning around and riding back," he said.

"Then it's settled, we have a deal," Alberta said.

"We have. Do we shake on it?" he asked.

"I've something better in mind," Alberta said, and the lavender eyes were suddenly darkened. She moved toward him as, with one hand, she pulled the buttons at the neck of the long nightdress open. The top of the dress fell away and she moved her shoulders, a little wriggling motion, and the nightdress slid to the floor to bunch around her ankles. Alberta faced him absolutely naked, her eyes glinting with tiny, dark pinpoints, and he let his eyes move up and down her body as she stood before him. It wasn't the body of an absolutely stunning woman, but that of a woman that still retained enough of her beauty, a woman with determination and desire, which made mere flesh more than it was. Her long breasts fairly quivered and hung down in twin concave curves until they filled out at the bottoms and pushed out brownish little nipples. A long figure balanced itself well, broad, rounded shoulders and broad, rounded hips, a tight abdomen, and an outward curve of a fleshy belly that came down to a densely appealing black tangle. Below it, long legs that would have done credit to a sixteen-year-old, smooth and unblemished, with thighs long enough to take the thin layer of extra flesh they wore.

But even naked, Alberta refused to be vulnerable: she faced him with the control and authority that sought to deny her nakedness and made desire a demand. He smiled inwardly. He'd been right in waiting to let her make the first move, but now it was time to let her know he wanted inner as well as outer nakedness. She reached out to him, began to unbutton his shirt as he tossed his gun belt aside and pulled at his trousers. His shirt came off and he quickly matched her nakedness and saw her eyes flick down at his powerful manhood. But Alberta held back the gasp that rose involuntarily to her parted lips; she pressed both hands against his chest and he let himself fall back onto the bed as she pushed. She came down half atop him and reached down for him. He let her touch the rigid spear of flesh for an instant and then pushed her from him. "No, let me," Alberta said, the demand in her voice.

"When I want you to, honey," Fargo said, and rolled her on her back. He felt her body stiffen for an instant, hands push against him in protest, but he bent forward, curled his lips around one long breast, and drew it into his mouth. He pulled, tongued, sucked the soft mound, not roughly, yet not with gentleness, and the brownish nipple rose at once, pushed against his tongue. He caressed the little point, sending his tongue around its tiny protuberance and he heard Alberta's breath draw in sharply. "Ah . . . ah . . . oh," she uttered, and he felt her hand move down his body, reaching for him again.

"Let me," she said, and the authoritive demand was still in her voice.

"When I want," he returned, shifted, pulled hard on her breast, and she gave a little cry, half-pain, half-pleasure. He brought his muscled body over her and pressed his pulsing, seeking eagerness between her thighs, and her hands tightened against him as she spread her legs open at once.

"Go . . . go in . . . ah, go in," Alberta said, but he pushed the tip of his organ to the dark, warm entrance. "Go . . . go . . ." she cried, her voice rising in demand. But he stayed, just touched the soft, lubricious lips with the pulsing tip of his maleness. "Go in, go in . . . damn you, Fargo . . . go in," Alberta cried. He moved, rubbed a brief moment of sensory ecstasy, and stayed. "Oh, oh, go in . . . oh," Alberta cried out as she lifted her hips, tried to ram herself forward around him. But he drew back with her while he kept the pulsing tip against her. "Oh, Jesus, please . . . please, Fargo . . . please," Alberta Farrow cried out, and suddenly there was only imploring in her voice, a half-sob of desire.

He slid forward into her warm, dark moistness and her half-scream was a sigh of grateful wanting. She lifted her long thighs, clasped them around his hips instantly. "Now, please, now . . . oh, God, please, oh, Jesus . . . yes, yes . . . aaaah," Alberta breathed as he began to move inside her, thrustings that grew hard and fast quickly as she clutched at him, legs tightened around him, arms pulled his face down to hers. He kissed her as he thrust harder into her, let his tongue echo his every movement, and between breaths Alberta emitted tiny little screams.

The tiny screams began to merge, became one long wail as he moved faster inside her. "Fargo . . . Fargo . . . aaaaaiiiii . . . oh, oh, Fargooooooo . . ." Alberta cried out, and he felt the long breasts falling back and forth against his chest as he tossed her body beneath him. With unexpected suddenness her fingers dug into his back and her tangled black triangle rose to push against his belly. She lifted, quivered, and buried her mouth into his chest as she screamed, a long, wailing, sobbing sound that ended only when she fell back, arms and legs dropping away from him as though they were suddenly lifeless. She lay breathing heavily and he kissed the ends of the long breasts gently and she gave a tiny gasp. He rolled to her side and lay against her, pushed himself onto one elbow, and enjoyed the long, earthy loveliness of her. She finally shook herself and sat up, and the lavender eyes stared at him.

"Satisfied, boss lady?" he asked mildly, but her eyes told him she caught the thin edge of sarcasm in his words.

"Quite," she said. "For now."

"Sure beats shaking hands over a deal, I'll admit," he said.

"Doesn't it?" she remarked, and reached out for the nightdress that lay beside the bed. Her long breasts brushed over his chest and the touch sent a current of excitement through him. He reached out, pulled her back, his hands closing over both breasts.

Alberta Farrow turned to him at once. "Jesus," she murmured as her mouth fell onto his hungrily. Her hand reached down, paused, and he laughed inwardly and shifted, pushed himself forward for her. She closed her fingers around him as he quickly grew, thickened, began to pulsate. "Oh, Jesus, yes, please, please," she murmured as she bent her head down to him. He lay back in answer and felt her lips on him, caressing, kissing, enclosing, and she murmured tiny sounds of pleasure. He took her again when he wanted, and she came to him with willing, eager compliance, wanting wiping out all else, only the demands of desire part of her now.

When she finally lay beside him again, her long body still quivering, she drew in deep breaths of air until finally she pushed herself up onto one elbow and saw his eyes studying her. "What are you thinking?" Alberta asked. "About Abram?"

"No," he answered without hesitation. "You've your reasons for being here. That's enough for me."

"Good." She smiled. "I hate explanations." She rose, swung the nightdress up and over her shoulders, and let it fall to the floor. "Yakes will get everything ready tomorrow. You'll head out the next morning, seven men and one chuck wagon," she said as she paused at the door.

He nodded and she slipped from the room with a quick, graceful move. He turned the lamp out and stretched his long frame across the bed, Alberta lingering in his thoughts. She had surprised him with her openness about Janet. But Alberta Farrow was a quick-minded, clever woman. She'd know when admission was more effective than silence. He'd learned little more than he already knew about Alberta . . . even in bed, he thought, smiling.

He closed his eyes, had started to slip into sleep when his wildcat's hearing caught the sound outside, horses slowly coming to a halt. He unfolded his long frame from the bed and stepped to the window, from where he could see the front of the house. Two riders were helping Owen Farrow from his horse and he watched the young man slide to the ground, collapse onto his knees, and sway there for a moment. Owen Farrow tried to get up and toppled drunkenly to one side.

"How many times we gonna have to do this?" Fargo heard one of the men ask. "He loses heavy and then drinks himself blind."

"We do what the boss tells us to do," the other answered. "Let's go. Ed said to bring him home, not tuck him in."

Fargo heard the other laugh as they rode away and he stayed at the window and watched Owen Farrow try to pull himself to his feet, topple over again, and settle for his hands and knees. The man crawled that way into the house and Fargo turned from the window with his eyes narrowed in thought. Gambling was more than an occasional pastime with Owen Farrow. Fargo had seen the type often enough: men driven by an inner need, men who'd beg, borrow, steal, and kill to feed their habit. Owen Farrow had revealed a new reason for him to protect his source of income, the kind of reason that made men forget everything but themselves.

Was Owen Farrow that kind? he wondered. It looked too much that way, Fargo mused as his thoughts tumbled on. So far there had been no direct attack on Janet, only attempts to scare her off, as she'd put it. That fitted Owen Farrow also. It wasn't likely he'd be able to bring himself to do in his own sister. Not likely, Fargo repeated, and grimaced as the weakness in the words. Lots of not-likely things came to pass. Too many. How far would selfishness and desperation drive Owen Farrow? he pondered.

He turned on his side and closed his eyes. He'd pay Janet one more visit, come morning. Perhaps it was time she stopped looking in only one direction. Maybe her family was more than just upset with her. She ought to think more about it, no matter how much the thought hurt. He'd tell her and be done with it. The rest was up to her. Pushing aside further thought, he let himself sleep.

4

He'd let himself sleep a little longer than usual and he walked down the hallway after he'd washed and dressed, headed for the kitchen to find a cup of coffee. He halted as he heard Yakes first, then Alberta, the man's voice with an added note of surliness.

"I still don't like it," Yakes growled. "I told you I could do all of it, breaking a new trail, leading the drive, and now you've got him running back here with the payroll. I don't like it."

"I want you to stay with the men, Yakes, make sure they're in shape to come back when the week is up," Alberta said almost soothingly. "I'm doing what I think is best, remember that."

Yakes refused to be placated, his voice dark. "You need me, remember that. I know what's going on around here," he said.

Fargo heard the sweet acid come into Alberta's voice. "Perhaps it was a mistake to have you help me in certain confidential things, Yakes. You seem to have forgotten who's running the Double-C," she said.

"I didn't mean that. I didn't mean anything bad," Yakes said, backing down at once, apology quick in his voice. Fargo heard Alberta walk firmly from the house and the foreman follow. He waited a moment more and then made his way to the kitchen, the exchange hanging in his thoughts. Alberta had spoken of confidential things. Had those things to do with Janet? he wondered. Everything at the Farrow ranch seemed shrouded in hidden meanings. He found the coffeepot bubbling, poured himself a mug of the hot, bracing brew, and wondered how widespread the hidden meanings reached. He'd finished half his mug of coffee when Owen Farrow came into the room and headed for the coffeepot. Owen looked a lot fresher than Fargo would have expected, the big man observed. Only a thin network of red lines in his eyes gave evidence that he had been staggering drunk only a few hours back. Youth, Fargo thought.

"Saw Alberta a little while back," Owen Farrow said, peering over the rim of his mug at the big man. "She told me about your helping Janet. Seems we misjudged Sis," he said.

"Seems so," Fargo echoed.

"You got her ear?" Owen asked.

"Maybe," Fargo answered, curious at the question.

"Tell her to give up this idea of hers. Nobody wants it. She's wasting her money, and her time, and now, it seems, her neck," Owen Farrow said.

"You talking as part of the Double-C or as a brother?" Fargo smiled slowly.

"Both," the younger man said with a note of swagger in his voice.

"I'll try, but I don't think she's going to listen much to me," Fargo said. "How are those deals of yours coming on?"

"Fine, just fine," Owen said as he finished his coffee and rose. "Talk to Sis. For her own good," he added as he walked from the kitchen, drawing the swagger around himself.

Fargo thought for a moment as he drained the mug and finally walked from the house. Yakes and Seth Bailey were near the Ovaro and Bailey smiled in greeting. Yakes gave him a surly stare.

"We'll be heading out at daybreak," he muttered.

"Good enough," Fargo said, and climbed onto the Ovaro. He rode out at a fast trot, distanced himself from the ranch before he turned and headed for Janet's place. His eyes swept the stand of red cedars as he rode past, but nothing moved. He reached Janet's place with the sun still not in the noon sky. Bixby Bunker had the calf in the front yard and was busy examining its hooves when Fargo rode to a halt.

"She's inside, getting her gear together," Bixby said, not interrupting his work, and Fargo swung to the ground.

"She going somewhere?" he asked.

"She'll tell you," the old man said. "Thought she had."

The front door of the house hung open and Fargo went inside to see Janet stuffing a pair of saddlebags. "Hello," she said. "This saves me the trouble of looking for you. What brings you out here?"

"Advice and messages," he said.

"Start with the advice."

"Don't only look Barnaby Tilden's way," Fargo said. "Your kid brother seems real bothered by what you're doing."

Janet frowned at once. "You saying my brother could be out to kill me?" she snapped.

"Maybe just to scare of you off, as you said. But mistakes happen," Fargo replied. "They've happened before."

"Nonsense. Maybe Alberta, but not Owen," Janet returned almost angrily.

"He told me to tell you to give up the idea. Nobody wants it, he said, and you're risking your neck," Fargo told her.

"He's just being concerned over me," Janet said with a tiny frown.

"Hope so," Fargo said. "You believe whatever you want. I've said my piece. Now, why were you coming to look for me?"

"First, to tell you I've a job for you, real good money," she said. "There are two Charolais calves waiting for me in Dodge City, younger than the one outside, two months old each. I'll pay you to help me get them back safe. Two hundred dollars, Fargo."

"That seems the going rate around here," Fargo commented.

"What do you mean?" Janet frowned.

"I'm spoken for. Alberta hired me last night, same rate," he told her. "I'm sorry."

"Hired you for what?" Janet snapped.

"To turn around and rush the payroll back to her. Seems she needs it right away," Fargo said. "There's no way I can help you out. Herding two young calves will be a long, slow haul with plenty of stops to rest them."

"She made that deal on purpose, to keep you from helping me get those two calves back safe," Janet spit out.

"You jumping to conclusions again?" Fargo asked.

"No, I know that's what she did," Janet snapped.

"She know you'd be going to pick up those calves?" Fargo questioned.

Janet's lips tightened for an instant. "She knew I'd ordered them. She didn't know exactly when I'd be picking them up."

"So you're just talking wild," Fargo said.

"No, I'm not. I know her. That's the way she operates. She didn't take any chances. When she heard about your helping me last night, she made sure you wouldn't be doing it again," Janet insisted.

Fargo turned her words in his mind. She was full of anger, suspicion, and defensiveness. He couldn't embrace her angry accusations but he couldn't dismiss them entirely either, and he swore under his breath. Alberta had been open about her displeasure with Janet, disarmingly so, he remembered, but she was also quick-minded enough to have done what Janet accused her of doing. Damn, he swore again inwardly. "You've no proof and I can't go along with a lot of wild talk," he growled.

"You're being used," Janet flung at him.

"If so, I guess I'll find out in time. It's been done before," Fargo answered.

"Tell her you can't do it. Tell her you're going to help me," Janet said with lofty disregard for everything but her own desires.

"No, I made a deal. I don't go back on my word," Fargo said sharply.

The green-flecked eyes continued to blaze. "Of course not, especially when she gave you a bonus for it," Janet snapped waspishly. "Go on, tell me she didn't add something special to the deal."

"I'm not saying yes, no, or amen, honey," Fargo growled.

"You don't have to, I know her," Janet said with disdain. "Well, you can be sure I'm not offering any bedroom bonus."

"Not even if you wanted to?" Fargo slid at her.

"No, not even then, and I don't want to," Janet threw back.

"No matter." He shrugged. "I made a deal. I'll stick by it."

"By all means," Janet said. "For a little while last night I thought maybe you cared about right and wrong. I see I was mistaken."

"I did my share of helping you last night. You want more than you've a right to ask," Fargo told her. She kept her pugnacious little face set, but the flicker in her eyes told him he'd hit on target. He strode from the house as she wrapped herself in angry silence. Outside, Bunker Bixby watched him ride away, his weathered face troubled.

Fargo turned north in a wide circle and pulled his jacket closed to the biting wind. A pattern of high, gray-white puffball clouds moved across the sky from the north. Winter clouds, he'd always called them, silent messengers echoed by the sharpness of the wind below. He turned the Ovaro slowly back toward the Farrow ranch in the afternoon sun, which had begun to lose its warmth.

Dissatisfaction still rode with him. He could understand Janet's quick-tempered accusations. They came out of anger and fear. But that didn't make them right. Yet he wondered if he were indeed being used. That didn't bother him as much as sitting on top of a whirlpool and being sucked in by it. He'd be happy to break trail, finish his agreement with Alberta, and be on his way. But he rode with the uneasy feeling that it wouldn't be that simple, and almost as if to confirm his thoughts, he saw the cloud of dust appear to his left; then the riders appeared driving a herd of young whiteface steers.

They headed for a small stream that crossed southward, he saw. He turned the Ovaro and rode toward the men as they reached the stream and let the young stock drink their fill. Six cowhands, he counted, led by a large man, a heavy body sitting atop a heavy brown horse, a red vest hanging open over a tan shirt. Fargo saw one of the cowhands ride over to the burly man as he reined the Ovaro to a halt. The man peered at him out of a hard-jawed face with blue eyes to match. A prominent nose and a large jaw balanced each other in a face that carried authority in its every line.

"You're Fargo," the man called.

"How'd you know?" Fargo asked.

"One of my boys was at the Silver Garter last night," the man said. "I'm Barnaby Tilden." Fargo let his eyes nod back. "You're real fast, I'm told," Barnaby Tilden said.

"Most times," Fargo allowed.

"You'd best be if you're working for Janet Farrow," Tilden said. "A lot of folks are real bothered by her ideas."

"You're one of them, I hear," Fargo said.

Barnaby Tilden's heavy jaw tightened. "I know the things she's been saying about me since that cowhand of hers was killed. Real little bitch, that one," the man rasped. "You're a damn fool to work for her."

"I'm not. I'm working for Abram. Just happened to be on hand last night."

Barnaby Tilden's eyes narrowed as he stared at the big

man on the gleaming black-and-white horse. "You believing the things she says?" he questioned.

"Can't say yet. My business, in any case," Fargo answered.

"I don't like being called a backshooter. I don't like anything Janet Farrow's trying to do. I'll do my damnedest to stop her, but I wouldn't go killing over it," Tilden said.

"I'll remember that," Fargo said blandly.

Barnaby Tilden swung his horse around. "Stay away from her, Fargo. She's trouble. Folks hereabout won't take kindly to you helping her," he said as he waved to his men and the cowhands began to move the young steers away from the stream.

Fargo watched the hard-jawed man ride away with his brow furrowed. Had Barnaby Tilden flung out simple advice, he mused, or a threat cloaked as advice? The man had the kind of harshness to fight to win, that was plain in his hard eyes. He'd been quick to say he wouldn't go as far as killing, but then, Fargo smiled grimly, he couldn't be expected to admit differently.

Barnaby Tilden and the pack of young steers disappeared in the distance and Fargo steered the Ovaro to a small cluster of red ash and dismounted. The last of the day was slipping over the horizon as he sat down against a tree trunk and pulled the collar of his jacket up to ward off the cold wind. He sat motionless and let the night lower across the land. He knew it was curiosity more than anything else that pushed at him.

He wanted another look at Barnaby Tilden. Somebody had lost three men last night. If it had been Tilden, there ought to be some signs, Fargo reasoned, bunks with gear waiting for occupants, maybe empty saddle pegs in the stable. He'd try and see for himself if Alice

Calkin or Janet Farrow were right about Barnaby Tilden.

He let the moon slowly rise into the cold of the night before he pulled himself onto the Ovaro. A north wind blew sharply and he felt an edge of dampness in the air, harbingers of an early snow. The first snow could come as a brief white messenger of the fury that was winter, or it could sweep down as winter's first paralyzing blow. He'd seen it both ways, and he could only hope for the first and was glad he'd be heading south, come morning.

The tracks of Tilden's steers were easy to follow in the moonlight and he rode at a fast trot until the half-frozen buildings came into sight. He saw a small knot of buckeyes and steered the Ovaro to the last of the trees, which was some twenty-five yards from the buildings. Dismounting, he let his gaze take in the corrals that stretched out on three sides of the buildings: at least a half-dozen large corrals and as many smaller ones. Some held young whiteface and young longhorns. He counted eight buildings, the main house, the bunkhouse, and six barns. He moved forward in a crouch and neared the barns first. One smelled of hogs, one of horses, and the others of cattle.

He made his way to the bunkhouse, where a dim, wavering glow touched the window. He halted below the window, straightened up enough to carefully peer over the weathered sill. The dim, wavering light, he saw, came from a lone candle that burned in one corner of the bunkhouse to give out a flickering night-light. He slowly scanned the rows of bunks inside the room, two of them double bunks. He counted fourteen bunks. Seven had sleeping forms in them and seven were empty, but two had clothing strewn atop them. That left five without any personal possessions. The numbers didn't add up right, but then maybe Tilden didn't have enough hands to fill every bunk. He slowly scanned the bunkhouse again as the lone candle continued to flicker, and his gaze came to an abrupt halt when he reached the far corner. Three canvas bags were on the floor, one beside the other in a neat row, each tied closed, each plainly full. He stared for a moment longer, three canvas bags that had obviously been set aside.

His brow furrowed as he crouched down again and made his way to the stable, where the distinct smell of horses drifted into the night air. He pulled the door open to let the moonlight into the front part of the stable. The horses sensed his presence at once and he heard nervous movements, hooves pawing at the ground, the soft slap of manes being tossed. He stayed quietly and let the horses calm down, grow used to him, before he moved into the stable. The moonlight outlined a double row of stalls and he squinted in the dimness as he moved past the stalls. Finally he found what he sought, the wall with the saddle pegs. He quickly strode to it and his eyes swept the saddles hanging there. He counted ten saddles, each in its own place. Three pegs, interspersed with the others, were empty, the three saddles obviously missing. Three missing saddles and three canvas bags waiting in the bunkhouse. Fargo frowned as he let thoughts race. It still didn't fit properly.

Had Tilden already discovered his three men in the cedars? If so, he'd have guessed what had happened and he'd have been quick to get rid of their personal belongings, not have them packed in bags as if waiting to be picked up. He'd have put their saddles back in place, too. Saddles cost too damn much to throw them away on a working cattle spread.

It fit and yet it didn't, Fargo grimaced, and the

thought had just revolved in his head when he heard the hoofbeats, Barnaby Tilden's voice following immediately. "He's here someplace. Find him, goddammit," Fargo heard the man shout. "Get the rest of the boys out of the bunkhouse."

Fargo cursed as he dropped into a crouch and heard footsteps running toward the bunkhouse. He peered back to where he'd left the stable door open to let the moonlight in and he cursed under his breath. He hadn't figured on Barnaby Tilden being out, probably in Rock Hollow, but the man had returned and obviously spotted the Ovaro beside the buckeyes. He receded deeper back into the stable and began to edge back of one row of stalls when he heard Tilden's voice again. "Over there, the stable door," the man shouted. "Come on. The boys will be here in a minute."

Fargo halted, listened, heard the sounds of two men running forward. He waited and heard them race into the stable, one going to the right, the other to the left. He crept forward along the line of stables as he listened to the two men searching, moving with quick, darting steps. "He's in here," Tilden's voice said from across the stable, and Fargo halted at the edge of an empty stall, stepped inside it, and dropped to one knee. He edged himself into the nearest corner as the cowhand searching on his side neared. The man was halting to peer into each stall, Fargo heard, and he drew the big Colt to grip it by the barrel. The others would be racing from the bunkhouse in moments. He'd have but one chance and he had to make it count. He didn't want a shoot-out, not yet, not with so many questions still hanging fire, and he sure as hell didn't want to find himself with a rope necktie as a thief.

He crouched low, every powerful muscle drawn tight

as the man halted outside the next stall, paused, peered in past the horse, which moved nervously. Fargo heard the man move on and saw the dark shape halt at the entrance to the empty stall. The man's gaze moved over his head to the rear of the stall first, and Fargo had counted on his doing just that. He came up from where he crouched at floor level, swinging the big Colt in an upward arc. The butt of the gun smashed into the man's forehead and Fargo heard the skin tear and saw the spurt of dark red that leapt outward as the dark shape collapsed with a gasped groan.

"Harry?" Fargo heard Tilden call, and he reversed his grip on the Colt as he streaked past the form that lay on the stable floor. He skirted the edge of the stalls and bolted from the stable only to skid to a halt as he saw the figures tumbling out of the bunkhouse, some clad only in long johns but all with guns in hand. Fargo dropped low again, stepped back, and pressed himself against the outer wall of the stable as he edged around the nearest corner. "In here," he heard Tilden call out. "Get a lamp lighted."

Fargo stayed crouched against the side wall of the stable and listened to the men race inside. He waited a moment longer and then scurried along the wall till he reached the end of the structure. He could see the Ovaro at the edge of the buckeyes and he heard the voices shouting inside the stable as a filtered flicker of lamplight reached out through the cracks between the boards of the wall. They'd realize he'd slipped out in moments, he grimaced. He had to make a run for it. Digging heels into the ground, he streaked across the open space toward the Ovaro. He'd just vaulted into the saddle when he saw the figures running out of the stable, fanning out to search the ground nearby. He flattened himself low over the horse's withers as he backed the Ovaro into the buckeyes. He moved the horse slowly till he reached the center of the small cluster of trees, then sent the animal into a trot as he wove his way through the remainder of the thicket. When he emerged on the other side, he let the horse stretch out into a full gallop.

Tilden would know he'd given them the slip by now, but neither he nor any of his men had actually seen him. But Tilden wasn't likely to give up without trying to run him down, and Fargo kept the Ovaro running hard until he'd crossed two low hills and was satisfied he'd put enough night between him and anyone trying to find him. He slowed, let the Ovaro draw in deep drafts of air, and turned his collar up against the sharp bite of the night.

Thoughts turned in his mind as he rode back toward the Farrow spread. Three men were plainly missing from Barnaby Tilden's place. Maybe it did fit right, after all. Maybe Tilden was a man of contradictions, Alice Calkin and Janet both right about him. He had seen it before, good and bad all wrapped up together. One man, two faces. The thought remained as the darkened buildings of the Farrow spread came into sight. He rode to the stable, unsaddled the Ovaro, and made his way into the house and the guest room.

He smiled as he reached the door and pushed it open, the tall figure waiting there confirming the wager he'd made with himself. Alberta caught the tiny smile on his lips as he closed the door.

"Grown sure of yourself very quickly, haven't you?" Alberta said testily.

"No. Sure of you," Fargo said.

Alberta's eyes searched his face as she stepped closer and Fargo saw the anger in the tightness of her mouth.

"Why didn't you come back sooner, then?" Alberta said. "Been out helping Janet again?"

"No, just scouting around some," Fargo answered mildly.

"Dammit, I can't stay any longer now. Abram's been restless these nights. He keeps waking up. I've got to get back," Alberta glowered.

"Too bad," Fargo commented.

"Is that all you can say—dammit?" Alberta bristled.

"That'll do," Fargo said as her arms slid around his neck. Her lips were parted as she pressed herself against him, her mouth closing over his, her tongue darting forward.

"Hurry back," Alberta breathed. "I need more than that payroll, Fargo. God, much more."

"I'll do my best," he said, and let one hand close around the full bottom of one long breast. Alberta shuddered, clung to him a moment longer and then wrenched herself away. She slipped from the door, her glance a mixture of accusation and wanting. He listened to her hurry away before he shed clothes and lay down across the bed. Maybe Janet had been right about why Alberta had hired him to return the payroll, but maybe that was unimportant now. Had Barnaby Tilden's three missing men held the real answer? He fell asleep with the question still hanging.

The new day slipped through the window to wake him; he washed and dressed, found hot coffee in the kitchen, and downed a solitary mug. The shouts of cowhands emptying the corrals of steers greeted him as he stepped outside and he saw Abram there, watching, Alberta beside him. Fargo felt her eyes on him as he went to the stable to return with the Ovaro saddled. Alberta had positioned herself behind Abram and her eyes met Fargo's glance as her lips silently formed the words *hurry back*.

He nodded at her, swung onto the Ovaro, and rode away, passing the long line of steers. The whiteface seemed to stick together, he noted, and Seth Bailey waved at him as he passed. At the head of the herd, Yakes only threw a surly glance at him, and Fargo put the Ovaro into a trot. He headed southeast, quickly leaving the slow-moving herd. He'd crested a low hill when he saw the five horsemen riding hard toward him, Barnaby Tilden in the lead, his red vest unmistakable. Fargo reined to a halt and his hand rested lightly on the Colt .45 at his hip as the riders reached him. He saw Barnaby Tilden's eyes take in his hand on the gun, but the anger stayed in the man's heavy-jawed face.

"I heard Abram was driving cattle today. I figured you'd be there," Barnaby Tilden said. "What were you doing sneaking around my place last night?"

"You see me there?" Fargo asked.

"I saw your horse, goddammit," Tilden roared.

"He's not the only Ovaro around," Fargo answered.

"Don't you try to fast-talk me, you bastard," Tilden flung back. "It was you, all right."

"Not's so's you can prove," Fargo insisted.

"Maybe I can't prove it, but I know it. What'd you come looking for, dammit?" Tilden shouted.

"Maybe you were the one that was out looking," Fargo said blandly, and saw Tilden frown at him.

"Looking for what?" the man said.

Fargo half-shrugged. "Three missing hands," he said, and saw both surprise and wariness creep into Tilden's face.

"I'm not missing anybody. Three of my men quit last

week. Got an offer twice what I was paying them, they said," Tilden answered.

"Doing what?" Fargo pressed.

"They didn't say. They just took off in a hurry. I expect they'll be back for the rest of their things," the man said.

"Don't count on it," Fargo said. Tilden stared at him, his eyes narrowing, and Fargo saw him sorting thoughts in his mind.

"What are you up to, Fargo?" Tilden asked.

"Breaking trail for Abram Farrow's drive," Fargo said.

Barnaby Tilden studied him for a few moments longer, his eyes still narrowed. "See that's all it is," the man growled ominously. "Come sneaking around my place again and you're a dead man."

Fargo let the threat go unanswered and watched the man ride angrily away. Barnaby Tilden had been quick to explain away the three missing men. Too quick, Fargo wondered. But he could just have been telling the truth, the Trailsman realized. It would explain the three canvas bags packed and set aside. If his answers had been the truth, Janet was watching the wrong coyote. If . . . He moved the Ovaro forward and pushed away further speculation. He had a trail to break. He'd let others find the truth.

He continued to ride southeast along a dip in the land that grew into a shallow valley. It offered a broad avenue with natural sides to keep the herd together. Steers seldom climbed hillsides unless there was a damn good reason for it. In addition, the long, low valley headed in the direction of the Platte River which they could follow south across the corner of Missouri Territory and into Kansas.

He turned finally and rode back to meet Yakes and

the herd. He quickened his pace as he came in sight of the long, low, shapeless mass that finally sorted itself out into the slow-moving line of cattle. He saw Yakes riding midway down the far side of the herd and he felt his brows pull into a frown as he spotted the lone figure riding near the herd of the cattle, the roan mare trotting easily along a line of sedges. He put the Ovaro into a canter and the frown was still dug into his forehead as he pulled up before Janet Farrow. She regarded him with cool loftiness.

"What the hell are you doing here?" he asked.

"I'm going to pick up my calves," she said.

"By riding along with the drive?" Fargo queried.

"Exactly. I decided it'd be safer—slower but safer. I'll have to be going it alone on the way back," she said, and let the reproof lay in her voice.

"Yakes agree to this?" Fargo asked with some surprise.

"I'm a Farrow," Janet snapped with a flare of authority. "I can ride along on one of our drives if I feel like it. I don't need his permission." The flare of authority stayed in her eyes as she met his gaze. "And I didn't come to change your mind about helping me back," she sniffed.

Fargo smiled. "I say that?" he asked mildly.

"I don't want you getting the wrong idea," Janet responded with sarcasm.

"Wouldn't think of it." Fargo laughed and saw the temper flare in her eyes again.

"I don't want your damn help. You've got to run back to Alberta and collect another bonus in bed," Janet threw at him.

"You sound jealous." He laughed.

Her hazel eyes shot green-flecked fire. "You're mistaking contempt for jealousy," she returned, and cantered angrily away. Fargo rode to where Yakes and another hand were herding a dozen steers back into the herd.

"Take a right after the next hill, small dip in the land. You'll see it," the Trailsman said.

Yakes wore almost a sneer as his eyes flicked to Janet. "Alberta won't like her being along," he said.

"I didn't ask her to come," Fargo said.

"Alberta ain't going to believe that," Yakes said, and the sneer became tinged with triumph.

"You be sure and tell her," Fargo said, and turned the Ovaro away. He rode on, passed Janet without glancing at her, and followed the shallow valley to where it finally ended. He halted, his eyes on the ground where the marks of unshod Indian ponies crossed at the end of the valley. A low line of hills ran along southward and Fargo swept the tops of them with a long, slow gaze. But nothing moved, no bronzed forms coming into sight, and he dismounted, stretched out on the grass to wait for the herd.

Dusk had begun to move over the land as the cattle came into view, moving slowly down the shallow valley. He rose and moved to one side as Yakes and his men halted the herd, gathered up stragglers, and prepared for the night. The cook rolled the chuck wagon to the edge of the low valley and was quick to prepare supper as night fell. Yakes assigned two men for night watch and Fargo saw Janet sit down off by herself. He took a plate of beef stew from the cook and folded himself down beside Seth Bailey. Janet ate food she'd brought along in her saddle pack, he noticed.

"Feel sorry for her," he heard Seth Bailey comment.

Seth had been around a good while and Fargo decided to draw him out some. "Why?" he asked. "She's picked out a trail and she's got to follow it."

"Ever since her pa was hurt she's been sort of cut out," the man said.

"Alberta's got the inside track, it seems," Fargo offered.

"She sure has," the man agreed.

"What about Owen? He cut his sister out, too?" Fargo asked.

"He's only interested in himself," Seth Bailey said.

"Maybe she'll show them all they should've listened to her," Fargo said, but Seth Bailey only looked dubious. "You don't think she can do it," Fargo prodded.

"She's bitten off more than she can chew," the man said. "She and old Bunker can't build a herd and a new breed."

"You know Bunker?" Fargo asked.

"Too many years. Good man, but Father Time's leaning heavy on him," Seth Bailey said.

"Why don't you give her a hand? I'm sure she'd take you on," Fargo said.

"Always been loyal to Abram," the man answered. "Maybe if he stops running the Double-C I'll think about it. If she's still trying, then." He rose and returned his plate to the cook, and Fargo did the same. He took his bedroll and carried it away from the campsite to a small hillock that let him look down on the herd. He went to sleep with the soft sound of the cattle rustling in the background and the chill night air whispering of winter.

Dawn came in with a gray sky and a sharp wind, and he washed and dressed and went down to the chuck wagon, where the cook had a big, dented, two-quart coffeepot over a small fire. He took a tin cup of the hot liquid, had almost finished when Janet appeared, a deep-yellow shirt tight against the round, high breasts and a green kerchief around her neck. She allowed him a cool nod as she sipped her coffee.

Yakes appeared, the surliness ingrained, part of him morning, noon, and night, Fargo decided.

"This little valley ends in another mile or so on," Fargo told the man. "Turn south at the end of it. We'll go along the edge of the Platte. The herd can drink there, too."

"We let them drink and cross the river," Yakes said.

"Moving alongside will take us down through the corner of Missouri, a good, flat route," Fargo said.

"We won't make a penny's worth of time moving them alongside the river. They'll be stopping to drink every half-mile," Yakes answered.

Fargo turned the man's answer for a moment and nodded, the point well taken. Yakes knew his job. "All right, I'll go on ahead and find us another route," he said, finishing the coffee and striding to the Ovaro. He rode from the camp and reached the edge of the Platte; he paused as he scanned the slow-moving river. Yakes would bring the herd across where he stood, a narrow bend in the river that slowed any undercurrents that might be there. Fargo moved his horse into the river and crossed without the Ovaro having to swim for more than a few minutes. As he emerged on the other side, he heard the horse galloping up behind him and turned to see the deep-yellow shirt flash through a clump of tall pokeberry. He halted, waited, and watched her cross the river. Janet rode up to where he waited with some large spots of river water dampening the deep-yellow shirt, one almost exactly across the front of one high breast. It pressed against her to reveal the very round curve but not the slightest indication of a tiny tip.

"I got bored riding along with the herd," she said.

"You don't have to explain to me, honey," Fargo said.

"Didn't want you to get the wrong idea again," Janet said.

"Haven't done that yet." He smiled and her eyes narrowed, but she ignored the answer and brought the roan mare up to ride alongside him.

"It might've been wrong to give in to Yakes back there," she said.

"I gave in because he was right," Fargo told her.

"I know that, but he'll take it as a sign of weakness," Janet said.

"He can think whatever he likes, doesn't bother me any," Fargo answered. "I just want to get the job done the best and fastest way."

"You anxious to get away from here or back to Alberta?" Janet asked tartly.

"Now, that's none of your concern, honey," Fargo said.

"What if I asked you to stay on, come work for me?" she slid at him.

"Doing what? Raising cattle or keeping your hide in one piece?" He laughed.

"I don't know yet," she said.

"Ask me when you know," he said. "Meanwhile, you chatter. I've a trail to find." He spurred the Ovaro forward and Janet followed, caught up to him as he saw a long stretch of flatland that ran south beside a ridge of black walnut. He grimaced at the ridge of trees but the way below was too smooth and too straight to turn away from. He reined to a halt. His lips pulled back again as he saw the hoofprints on the ground. He dismounted and knelt down to run his fingers across the marks. Some crumbled to the touch, weeks old, but too many held the firmness of not more than twenty-four hours. He rose, let his eyes scan the territory to the west and east. Hills swelled, none steep, yet all high enough to slow the herd. The long stretch of flatland beside the ridge remained by far the best avenue.

"We'll take it," he said to Janet as she watched him. "There's not much chance in avoiding Indians if they're out to find you, anyway."

He stayed on the ground and Janet swung from her horse. "What now?" she asked.

"We wait for Yakes and the herd," he said, folding himself to the grass.

Janet sat down nearby, her hazel eyes studying him. "You're a funny man, Fargo," she said, and he waited. "You help when I don't ask you to, and don't when I do."

"It just came out that way. Or maybe you ask at the wrong times," he answered as he let his eyes idly move across the ridge of black walnut. He considered telling her what he'd found at Barnaby Tilden's and decided against it. She'd seize on it as confirmation of what she already believed, whereas he saw Tilden as a still unresolved question.

"What do you see in her?" Janet threw out with sudden vehemence, the question flung out of midair but its meaning unmistable.

"I've a contract to do a job for her," he answered.

"You know what I mean," Janet snapped.

"You don't get answers through the front door, you try the side. You don't give up, I'll give you that." Fargo smiled.

"I'm not looking for answers. I'm trying to understand you," Janet said angrily. "Don't you care that she's somebody else's wife—my father's, in this case?"

Fargo leaned back on one elbow. "Man gave me a theater ticket once. He said somebody else had bought it, paid for it, but wasn't using it. I didn't see any reason I shouldn't use it," he told her.

"A theater ticket and a woman aren't the same," she protested.

"That's right, you can get a refund on the first one if there's no performance," he said.

"Go to hell," she hissed, and got to her feet.

Fargo kept the smile inside himself as his eyes went to the sky. The afternoon shadows were starting to lengthen and he was glad when he saw the low cloud of dust that signaled the herd. Yakes rode up first, Seth Bailey beside him.

"Slow going crossing the Platte," Bailey said.

"We go straight south here," Fargo said to Yakes. "All the way to the Smoky Hill, I hope."

Yakes surveyed the area as the herd came up. "We'll camp for the night here, get a good start, come dawn," he said, and Fargo nodded agreement. He led the Ovaro down a hundred feet along the broad pathway as the herd spread out and began to settle down, the cowhands bringing in stragglers and wanderers. Fargo walked halfway up on the slope that led to the black-walnut ridge and peered down the broad passage. He saw a line of big-antlered elk crossing in the distance, then a half-dozen white-tailed deer. He dropped to one knee and continued to peer into the distance in the fading light. A pair of black bears came into his sight for a few moments and then disappeared behind thick brush. A soaring shape rose, dipped, became a bald eagle, and flew out of sight. Plenty of game, he noted. It was both a good and a bad sign. He'd found them a new trail into the Kansas Territory, plenty of fresh grass to cushion the long drive. The amount of game showed that. But that much game no doubt brought the Indian here. Automatically, his eyes swept the ridgeline again, but only the trees met his gaze. Maybe they'd get lucky, he told himself as he returned to the campsite, where the cook had supper on the fire.

Janet stayed off by herself again, he took note, plainly keeping away from Yakes. He ate quickly, leftover stew and hard bread, and passed her with his bedroll as he once again headed for the higher land. "I still don't understand you, Fargo," she muttered as he went by.

"Keep trying." He grinned and walked on. The night grew cold again, with the edge of winter in its sharpness. Abram Farrow had just sneaked under the wire with this drive, Fargo reflected as he stretched out on his bedroll. He slept quickly, aware through his sleep of the cry of coyotes and an occasional wolf far in the distance. He woke with the dawn, hurried to get coffee, and found Yakes had the men up and ready to ride.

"Move 'em out," Yakes called. "Keep 'em going. Let's make time today." Fargo saddled the Ovaro as he finished his coffee and was in the saddle as Janet rode up.

"I'll be riding on ahead," he told her as she gulped down coffee. He rode off at a fast trot, went into a canter as he skirted the steers. His eyes again swept the ridgeline as he moved on, but he saw nothing to bother him. He rode down the broad passage and saw that it widened in places, hosted two big box canyons that branched off to the right. He turned and started back when Janet rode up. "Yakes is driving them hard. He's not far behind," she said.

"Good," Fargo said, wheeled his horse around, and rode on again. He passed the first two box canyons and the ridgeline grew lower, the sloping side shallower. He'd gone on perhaps another mile when he saw the tall, bronzed, near-naked body of a lone horseman suddenly appear at the edge of the black walnut trees on the ridge. He heard Janet's faint gasp of surprise and fear. The Indian looked down at them and suddenly he was flanked by two more who seemed to appear magically from the trees. Two others followed, then a third. They sat as if carved in wood on their ponies.

Fargo caught the design on a wrist gauntlet one wore. "Sioux," he said. "Just keep riding slowly."

Janet edged her roan mare up alongside the Ovaro as she rode beside him, and he slowed to a walk and finally halted. The Sioux on the ridge had moved forward with them along the top of the ridge, and now they halted also. "What now?" Janet breathed.

"We wait for the others to catch up," Fargo said.

"I'm afraid," Janet murmured.

"Be afraid quietly," Fargo said softly. "Just sit your horse."

Janet nodded, drew in a deep breath that pushed the yellow shirt tight and made him wish he were someplace else with her. It seemed an eternity until Yakes and the herd came up and the Sioux hadn't moved from their position atop the ridgeline.

Yakes drew to a halt and followed Fargo's gaze. "Only six of them," the man muttered. "They're just lookin'."

"Maybe," Fargo said.

"No maybe about," Yakes said, and as he spoke, Fargo saw the other shapes emerge on the ridge. Two first, then three more, then four more. Fifteen altogether suddenly. He turned to Yakes.

"They're going to hit us," the Trailsman said quietly.

"Shit they are. Indians don't care about cows," the man said.

"They're going to hit us. Not yet, but when they're

ready. I'm going to ride ahead. You just keep moving till I get back," Fargo said.

"Ride wherever you want. They're not going to bother us," Yakes insisted with a sneer in his voice. "If you're scared, you just ride off and hide somewhere," he added.

Fargo's smile was tight as he wheeled the Ovaro around and rode on. He saw Janet start to go after him and waved her back. "You stay here," he said, and cantered on. He rode about a half-mile when he saw what he'd hoped to find: a narrow box canyon. He turned back to rejoin the others. Yakes halted the herd as he saw Fargo return and the Trailsman's glance went to the ridge. The Sioux were keeping pace with the herd, still lined single-file along the ridge. The one in the lead carried a lance, Fargo saw, the others with their short bows in hand.

"There's a box canyon up ahead. It'll be easier to reach than trying to turn the herd to go back to the ones we passed," Fargo said.

"What the hell for?" Yakes growled, and Fargo saw the other hands move up to listen.

"You'll drive the herd into it," Fargo said.

"You crazy? Drive the herd into a box canyon?" Yakes shot back.

"Those Sioux are going to attack. Out here, even if you manage to stay alive, you'll lose the herd. They'll scatter so far you'll never round them up again. They can't scatter in the box canyon."

"I told you, Indians don't give a damn about cattle. They're not going to hit us," Yakes insisted.

"They'll attack. Now, get those damn steers into that box canyon," Fargo said.

He saw Yakes thrust his jaw out. "You ordering me around?" the man growled.

"If I have to. I aim to save my own neck as well as the herd," Fargo said. "Move those steers, dammit."

"Go to hell. I'm runnin' this drive," Yakes said.

Fargo's eyes flicked to the others and saw uncertainty in their faces; Janet was wide-eyed with alarm. He swore silently. Yakes was being more than stupid and stubborn. He was going to show who was top dog, certain the results would find their way back to Alberta Farrow in time.

"Go along with me, Yakes. Take the herd into the canyon," Fargo said in an effort to head off a confrontation. He saw it was a waste of time as Yakes tossed him a grin of icy triumph.

"Go hide someplace. You're in my way," the man said. "I'm going on."

Fargo cursed under his breath again. Yakes gave him no choice. "I'm taking over. They go into the box canyon," Fargo said.

Yakes' eyes widened for an instant and he swung from his horse with a grin of anticipation across his heavy face. "We're gonna settle this right here and now," he said.

"Now, hold on, Yakes," Seth Bailey cut in. "This is no time for a private fight with all them Sioux looking on."

"I told you, they won't be bothering us," Yakes flung back at him as his eyes bored into the big man on the Ovaro. "You too yellow to get off that horse, Fargo?" he sneered. "Come on, let's see you take over."

Fargo uttered a deep sigh as he swung to the ground. "No, wait," he heard Janet call. "Maybe Yakes is right. I never heard of Indians caring about cattle. This is no time for trying to prove anything."

"I'm not here to prove anything. I just aim to keep my

scalp," Fargo said as he moved away from the horse to face Yakes.

"They won't want any part of you when I'm finished with you," Yakes growled, the sneering grin still on his face as he dropped his burly body into a half-crouch and came forward. He drew closer, raised his arms, shot out a quick left that Fargo sidestepped. He tried another and Fargo easily avoided it. Yakes still wore the tight grin of triumph as he tried a short right. Fargo brought up his arm to block the blow just as he realized it had been a feint and Yakes was diving in low, both arms outstretched. Fargo tried to twist to one side, but Yakes barreled into him just over the knees and he felt himself go down. Yakes, half atop him, brought a hammerblow up and over to land into his stomach, and Fargo knew that only the hard, trim muscles of his abdomen prevented the fight from ending right there.

As it was, he was left breathless and he gulped in air as Yakes pulled himself up and tried to wrap a thick arm around his neck. Fargo got one knee raised enough to bring it up sharply into his foe's belly. He heard Yakes grunt and the man's grip loosened for an instant. But an instant was enough, as Fargo brought a sharp, hard left up against Yakes' ribs and the man half-fell to one side. The Trailsman twisted away, rolled, and came up on his feet as Yakes pulled himself up. The sneer had vanished from the man's face, a snarl of fury in its place. Yakes came forward again, lighter on his feet than Fargo had expected he'd be. Fargo saw him try the right feint again, but this time the Trailsman's left shot out, a quick, straight blow, and Yakes' head snapped back. Fargo stepped forward with a right, but Yakes surprised him once more as he managed to pull away from the blow, go into the half-crouch again, and leap forward. He was both powerful and quick, and Fargo barely avoided the lunge as he twisted to the side. He lashed out with a short, upward left as Yakes plunged past him, but the blow only scraped alongside the man's head and Yakes spun around with a roar. He came forward again, both heavy fists upraised. He swung a left, a right instantly behind it, and Fargo gave ground as he parried both blows. Yakes swung again instantly, short, hard blows delivered with surprising quickness.

Fargo parried both, half-dropped, and came up under the last blow with a stinging left to the man's ribs. He heard Yakes grunt in pain, but the man spun around and threw a right cross that arced through the air. Fargo managed to take the blow against his shoulder as he ducked, but the force of it threw him off balance. He saw the left winging down at him, managed only to turn his head so that the blow caught him on the side of the face. He felt himself go down from the force of it and he saw Yakes there at once, the man's boot coming at him in a vicious kick. He rolled toward the boot instead of away from it, got one arm up around Yakes' ankle as the blow landed high against his chest. He yanked and the man went down. Fargo twisted the leg in his grip as he rose and heard Yakes yell in pain as he rolled free, scrambled, and regained his feet. But Fargo still felt pain in his face as he put his weight on his other leg.

Fargo moved forward, weaving now, and Yakes threw a roundhouse right and a left cross instantly after it. Fargo parried the right, ducked under the left, and drove his own right upward with all the strength of his powerful shoulders behind it. The blow caught Yakes almost full on the point of his jaw and he staggered backward, his eyes glazed for an instant. He was shaking his head when Fargo's ripping left hook struck. Yakes' head seemed to almost turn completely around and he sprawled sidways, fell, instinctively regained his feet. He swung, head down, but it was blind habit driving him now and Fargo brought up a whistling right uppercut. Yakes' head lifted, fell backward, and Fargo's follow-through left caught him flush on the jaw.

Yakes went down, rolled, wound up on his back to twitch for a moment and lie still. Fargo straightened, rubbed his knuckles against the side of his trousers, and looked up at the others. He started toward Seth Bailey and saw Janet to one side out of the corner of his eye. "Start moving them to that box canyon," he said to Seth Bailey.

"Yes, sir," the man replied.

"*Fargo!*" Janet's voice broke in as a knife cuts through air, and he heard the terror in it. He spun to see Yakes had come to, his face a blood-smeared snarl. The man had drawn himself up on one knee and he had his gun half out of its holster. Fargo's hand flew to the big Colt at his hip, the motion almost too fast for the eye to follow. The Colt barked twice as Yakes got his own gun up to fire. He managed to get off one shot, which whistled harmlessly skyward as he toppled backward, half-twisted, and fell sprawling with one leg twisted under him, the gun still clutched in his hand. He lay making little movements for a moment and Fargo saw his fingers finally fall open, the gun sliding from his lifeless hand. Fargo found himself thinking of Alberta's words about Yakes.

"He never understood his own limitations," Fargo murmured as he holstered the Colt. His eyes flicked to the ridge. The line of figures remained motionless, as if they'd been carved in wood and placed there. He returned his glance to Seth Bailey. "Take him to the side and cover him with some branches," he said. "We haven't time for more than that." He turned away and climbed onto the Ovaro as Janet came up, her hazel eyes round as they met his gaze. "I owe you one. He'd have shot me in the back," Fargo said.

Janet nodded, her round-cheeked face drawn tight as she mounted the roan. Seth Bailey waved a hand and Fargo saw the men start to move the steers forward. "How far to that box canyon?" Bailey asked.

"Quarter-mile or so," Fargo answered. "Move nice and easy till we get there. When I tell you, fire a shot and get those critters stampeding full speed into that canyon. Soon as the Sioux see what we're doing they'll come charging, but we ought to be inside by the time they reach us."

"We just hole up there?" Seth questioned.

"Hell, no. We fight. Get off your horses and use the steers as shields. They'll try to come in after us, but they won't be able to get a clear shot at anybody if we do it right," Fargo said, and spurred the Ovaro forward. Janet rode with him in strained silence and he saw the Sioux begin to move along the top of the ridge, keeping silent pace with the slow-moving procession below.

"What if they attack before we get to the box canyon?" Janet asked in almost a whisper.

"We're in a hell of a lot of trouble," he told her flatly. "But I don't guess they will. They watched the fight. They're curious now. They'll wait a spell to see what else might happen down here. They figure they can take us whenever they decide to do it."

He let his glance go up to the ridge without lifting his head and saw the line of bronzed figures continue to keep pace. He looked back and saw that Seth and the others were driving the steers with unhurried casualness. The passage opened on ahead, curved gently, and suddenly seemed a lot longer. He felt the thin line of perspiration across his forehead. Every second seemed an hour. The Sioux, he knew only too well, could decide to call off their cat-and-mouse game at any instant. He felt his sharp intake of breath as he suddenly spotted the tall wall of rock that marked the box canyon and he forced himself not to rush forward. He waited till he was within twenty-five yards of the entranceway before he turned and Seth met his glance. Fargo saw him bring four of the men up front at the left side to turn the steers and he saw the cook halt the chuck wagon and climb onto the horse tethered behind it. Two men stayed at the rear of the herd and Seth raised an arm, brought it down fast, and Fargo heard the two shots shatter the air from the rear of the herd.

The steers bolted at once, became a surging mass of hooves and hide, and the men in front fired their guns as they turned the stampeding cattle into the box canyon. Fargo's eyes went to the ridge and he saw the Sioux halt, the one in the lead lift his lance. As one, they began to race down the slope, but more than half the herd had already thundered into the cayon, Fargo saw, and the rest were racing in after them. "Ride," he shouted at Janet, and sent the Ovaro into the box canyon with the remainder of the steers. Those in front had already reached the stone end of the canyon and come to a milling halt; the others slowed, surged in a crosscurrent of restless calm. The last of the steers were into the narrow canyon, and Fargo saw the last two men leap from their horses amid the cattle. He drew the big Sharps from its saddle holster as he slid to the ground, sandwiched between his horse and two whiteface. He saw the rest of the men spotted throughout the packed herd. Janet, nearest him, stayed beside her roan mare. He returned his gaze to the entrance to the canyon as the Sioux charged in and pulled up as they saw the mass of cattle blocking their way.

Fargo fired and saw one Sioux topple from his pony. Three others fell as his shot was followed by a round of rifle fire from inside the packed cattle. He fired again at an Indian who started to wheel his horse and the Sioux pitched forward, clung for a moment longer before sliding off, his shoulder blades suddenly red. He saw the Sioux fire a hail of arrows more with frustration and anger than with aim. The one with the lance shouted, waved his long pole, and sent his pony galloping out of the canyon as the rest followed. One didn't make it to the entranceway as Fargo's shot blew the top of his head off. He listened to the Indians gallop out of sight and straightened his tall frame to peer across the mass of cows. "Anybody hit?" he called.

"No," a voice called back, and another added agreement. He saw Seth Bailey push his way through steers toward him.

"We got six by my count," Seth called. "You think the others took off?"

"No, the Sioux don't give up that fast," Fargo said. "But they won't try another charge." His eyes went up to the edge of rock that marked the top of the canyon. "They'll circle up there, crawl to the edge on foot. They'll count on us watching the entrance for them. Most folks not used to how the Sioux fight would be doing just that." Fargo paused, let his eyes scan both sides of the canyon rock. "Take three men and work your way to the right side. I'll take the rest with me to the left wall. You cover the top across from you and we'll cover the one across from us. Keep down behind the steers. Soon as they show, you fire."

Seth Bailey called out names and began to push his way through the steers toward the opposite wall of the canyon as Fargo motioned to Janet and began to move to the wall nearest him. He cursed at how long it took to go a few dozen yards through the densely packed steers, and Janet behind him, he used the butt of the rifle as a cattle prod to fight his way to the stone wall. He positioned himself with his back to the rock wall as the other men reached the stone and slid down behind the nearest steers, rifles pointed upward toward the top of the opposite wall. He had just reloaded the Sharps when the Sioux appeared, moving silently to the edge of the canyon wall, drawn bows in their hands. He saw them search the cattle for a moment, try to find the men among the steers. The rifle at his shoulder, Fargo fired and heard the fusillade of shots that resounded across the confines of the canyon. He felt himself knocked sideways as a big longhorn swung his rump around and the mass of cattle milled against one another at the sound that reverberated across the canyon. But he glimpsed the Sioux he'd held in his sights topple from the top of the rocks, two others pitching down split seconds later. As he lay with one hand over his head against the base of the canyon wall, he could hear the screams of Sioux as they toppled into the canyon.

The volley of shots ended and he heard only the sound of the steers rubbing and pawing nervously and then Seth Bailey's voice. "They've hightailed it, those that are left," the man called, and Fargo pushed himself to his feet, glanced around to see Janet huddled against the stone wall. He moved to her, helped pull her to her feet as he straightened up. "We got at least five more," Seth called.

"They won't be back this time," Fargo said. "Make sure nobody's hurt and then let's get the herd out of here." He made his way to the Ovaro, swung onto the horse, and pulled Janet into the saddle with him as he pushed his way to where her roan waited between two longhorns. She climbed onto her mare from the Ovaro and turned grave eyes on him.

"I still don't understand it, Sioux coming after cattle. How did you know they would?" she asked.

"They didn't give a damn about the cattle. Yakes was right about that. But they care about boots, guns, horses," Fargo said. "And they'd have liked taking you back to camp with them."

She gave a faint shudder and followed Fargo as he slowly moved the Ovaro through the steers. He reached the canyon entranceway and watched Bailey and the others expertly begin to drive the cattle out of the canyon, two hands moving up front to lead them out while the others prodded from the sides and the rear. The dusk shadows were stretching across the broad flat passage when the entire herd was finally out of the canyon. A dozen steers had arrows in them, most in the fleshy part of their rumps and the heavily muscled humps over their shoulders.

"We'll pull the shafts out when we make camp. We've got plenty of arrowroot and comfrey salve to put on the wounds," Seth Bailey said, and Fargo nodded as he rode ahead and found a place where the passage widened enough to make camp.

The night came quickly, the cattle tired and quieter than usual. The cook made supper and this time Janet stayed beside him as she accepted some of the camp food.   Fargo watched as she stared into the cooking fire, her round-cheeked face quietly pretty. "You're thinking hard," he observed, and she nodded.

"Thinking how we'd all be dead back there if Yakes had had his way and kept us out in the open," she said, shuddering. "It almost happened that way. It would have, except for you."

"Almost doesn't count," Fargo said. "And I still owe you."

The cook began to put out the fire and Janet rose, her face still grave, and as Fargo watched her, she suddenly seemed small and tired and troubled. The darkness of a night with the moon behind clouds swallowed her up and he laid out his bedroll and felt the weariness inside him as he stretched out. He lay awake for a few moments and let his mind turn thoughts, options, possibilities, until he finally grunted in satisfaction, turned on his side, and slept at once.

5

He woke before anyone else, with the very first hint of dawn touching the horizon, and rode on with the new day. When he returned to meet the others as they started to drive the herd forward, he'd charted the way southwest that took them below the Smoky Hill and avoided Abilene. Seth Bailey had taken leadership of the men with nobody objecting, and the herd moved smoothly. They'd made good time and it was midafternoon when they rested. Janet sat down beside him. The strain had left her pert face and she'd regained her usual sass, he noticed.

"How long before we reach Dodge City and you get to rush back to collect?" she asked.

"You're sounding jealous again." He laughed and received a quick glare. "Been thinking about you," he added, and a raised eyebrow replaced the glare. "I owe you. I'm going to help you get those two calves back," he said.

Her eyebrows went higher. "Surprise, surprise," she murmured. "What happened to keeping your word?"

"I figure to do that, too," he said, and she frowned at him.

"How?" Janet asked warily.

"Figured out a way to do both," Fargo told her. "You have enough money with you to buy a wagon? If not, I have."

"I've enough," she said.

"Buy one when we get to Dodge City, big enough to hold the calves. We'll put your calves in it, tie them right, and drive night and day. We'll spell each other and stop only to rest the horses. I figure we'll get back in just about the same time I'd take to do riding alone. I keep my word and you get your calves home safe."

She stared at him with a kind of wry admiration. "You do have your own code, don't you?" she said. "Strange as it is."

"I do it as I see it," he told her.

"And you still get to collect your bedroom bonus," she said.

"Maybe, but that's not your problem, honey," he said.

She suddenly seemed almost hurt. "I can't refuse," she said. "Or not be grateful."

"You can. It's a free country. You've got the right to be stupid," he answered.

"I'll get the wagon," she said, her face suddenly soft. "Thank you. Really."

"I'll get you back with the calves. The rest is all yours," he told her. "Let's ride."

She brought her horse up to ride beside him as he scouted the land until the dark came and they made camp.

"You expect more Sioux?" Janet asked over a supper of beans.

"No, and we're not west enough to run into Pawnee or Shoshoni. This is Oto, Iowa, and Kansas land, and none of them are in a class with the Sioux," Fargo said. "I'd guess they'd leave us alone."

She nodded, grateful for the reassurance, and as the days went by, his prediction proved correct because they saw only glimpses of distant Indian parties.

The long, hardworking days left no room for thoughts of anything but sleep when night came. But as the trail finally neared its end, Fargo noted that the smell of Dodge City—in the mind if not the nostrils—made the men grow anxious and restless. Even Janet grew excited with the prospect of picking up her two calves.

Dodge City, when they reached it, was as Fargo'd always known it—sprawling, brawling, undisciplined— the kind of place he called a saddle-sore town: full of cowpokes eager to be off a horse and on a woman. It was not a town he'd ever liked, Fargo thought as he watched Seth Bailey herd the steers into the marked stockades where the cattle buyers were waiting to count heads and pay the going rate.

"You'll stay on a spell with the men, I understand," he said to Seth, and the man nodded.

"I'll see they all get back when they've had enough funnin'," Seth said. "You did real well, Fargo. I figure you took four days off the usual time for the drive. Will I see you when I get back to the Double-C?"

"Not likely," Fargo said.

"Good luck to you, then," Bailey said.

"Same to you," Fargo returned, and walked to where Janet waited at the edge of one of the stockades. "Get the wagon and your calves. I'll meet you back here," he said, and watched her hurry through the crowds near the stockades. He found his way to the bank and had to cool his heels until he could hand the manager the letter Alberta had given him. The man, spectacled and prim-faced, consulted his boss with the letter and there were further delays while they checked Alberta's signature. Finally, the manager brought the payroll in a money belt, and Fargo signed for it and strapped it around his waist.

When he returned to the stockade area, he saw Janet with the wagon as she waved to him from the driver's seat. She'd gotten hold of an old Owensboro Texas cotton-bed wagon with the extra-high sides; they'd keep the calves in securely. He walked around the team hitched to it: two sturdy horses, part Morgan, with some draft-horse stock in them, powerful and heavy-legged. They'd stand up to the hard, steady pace with the endurance that would more than make up for speed.

"You did well," he said to Janet, and she flashed a delighted smile. He climbed onto the wagon and examined the two young calves.

"Aren't they beautiful?" Janet chortled.

"Nice," he agreed. "Healthy, strong, good shape. Now, let's get them to your place. I'll drive for now," He took the reins while Janet saw to the calves and secured them at the rear of the deep wagon. He retraced their path on the drive as he went north, and after they stopped to eat, Janet took the reins and he saw that she handled the heavy wagon well. He curled up inside the deep frame of the wagon and slept, to wake only when she halted to let the horses rest. When they started again, he took the reins while Janet slept, and it was near day when she woke to drive once more. The pattern established itself smoothly and the sturdy horses needed less rest than a lighter team would have while the Ovaro and the roan tied to the rear of the wagon had only to move along with riderless ease.

They made good time, and when they crossed back into Iowa, Fargo untied the Ovaro and rode scout for a few hours, guiding them in a wide circle to avoid a line of Sioux he spotted in the distance. When he returned to sit beside Janet in the wagon, the sun had begun to slip over the horizon. "Your time to sleep," he told her as he took the reins and shot a sharp glance at her. The fatigue had begun to show around her eyes and she crawled to the back of the wagon slowly. He drove into the night and finally pulled to a halt to break out some beef jerky and let the horses rest. Janet woke and clambered back to the driver's seat. She ate hungrily and he saw her rub the back of her neck. "I'm feeling it myself," he told her. "I've slept in more comfortable places."

"My bones are creaking," she said, spearing him with a sidelong glance. "I still don't understand you," she commented.

"Keep trying," he told her. "Your turn to drive." He climbed back into the body of the wagon, stretched his long frame as best he could, and tried to ignore the jouncing of the heavy wooden wheels as Janet spurred the horses forward. He woke just before dawn and took the reins again.

Luck stayed with them. Fargo spotted Indian pony tracks that circled away from them and only the dawn made him grimace as it came in gray and cold. Janet climbed back beside him, a blanket wrapped around her.

"Can't sleep," she said. "It's getting colder."

"Been doing that every few hours," Fargo said. He'd barely finished the sentence when a swirl of snowflakes descended and he saw the apprehension in Janet's face.

He watched the flakes for a few minutes. "No real force behind them," he said finally. "Just a little sample. We ought to reach your place by late afternoon."

"Thank God," she said, gratefulness and excitement mingling in her voice. He let her take the reins again, as she plainly didn't intend resting, and he got in another few hours of sleep. The sun had passed the noon sky when he woke and climbed onto the driver's seat beside Janet. Only a few snowflakes still fell, but the cold bit hard and he took the reins from her as she jammed her hands into her pockets. She glanced back at the calves with a worried frown.

"They're all right," he told her. "The sides are keeping the wind from them." She nodded, eager to be reassured, and he saw the determination behind the fatigue in her face.

She uttered a tiny sound of glee when her place came into view near day's end. Bunker Bixby ran from the house, amazement wrinkling his weathered face still further.

"I'll be damned. Didn't expect you for another week, at best," he said. "Hot damn, that must've been some trip."

"Luck rode along," Fargo said.

"I've hot coffee on," Bunker said. "I'll take care of that wagon and the calves."

"Coffee sounds wonderful," Janet said as she swung from the wagon with Fargo and led the way into the house. She flung off her jacket and poured the coffee as Fargo sank into a chair. He sipped the hot, bracing brew slowly and realized he felt more rested than he'd expected.

"Thank you, Fargo," Janet said, her hazel eyes suddenly grave.

"You've your new calves, but nothing else has changed," he reminded her. "You're still mighty unpopular with somebody."

"Maybe they'll give up when they see I won't," she said.

"Maybe," he allowed, unwilling to tell her that was more hope than sense. "I'll be getting that payroll to Alberta now," he said, finishing the coffee and rising to his feet. He saw Janet's eyes darken and words come to her lips, but she held them back. It was an effort, he thought, smiling inwardly.

"Will you be stopping back again?" she asked from the doorway. "Tomorrow, maybe?"

"Maybe," he said.

"Thanks again, for everything," she said as he strode to the Ovaro.

Fargo pondered her abrupt switch from flaring temper to almost little-girl humbleness. She was not a calculating woman, but she could pull a person into her problems and he'd had enough of that. He rode away telling himself Janet had been trouble from that first moment he'd met up with her, and he'd done more than enough helping.

Snow had begun to fall again as dusk turned into dark and this time he felt the sting of the flakes against his face. But it turned out to be only a hard flurry that ended as he reached the Farrow ranch. Only a lone light burned in the living room and he stabled the Ovaro and entered the house. Alberta appeared in the hall, a floor-length silk dressing gown of wine red wrapped around her tall figure. She put a finger to her lips.

"Welcome back," she whispered, the lavender eyes dark. "Abram's just gone to sleep. Wait for me in the guest room." He nodded, handed her the money belt,

122

and watched her turn and glide away, the silk gown clinging to her rear end. Alberta fairly simmered with wanting.

He smiled as he went down the hall to the room, closed the door behind him, and undressed. He stretched out on the bed and enjoyed its softness, but he found himself seeing Janet's pugnacious little face in his thoughts. She was simmering, too, he knew, but a different kind of simmering. Loyalty to her pa and plain female jealousy whirled inside her, even if she refused to admit the latter. He understood, even felt sorry for her, but hell, he wasn't about to turn away a night he'd earned on account of Janet's family feuds. He closed his eyes and let himself doze until he snapped awake at the sound of the door opening.

Alberta's tall figure came into the room and he watched her sink down on the edge of the bed, her eyes moving along his muscled nakedness. The silk dressing gown parted at the neck to reveal the long curve of one breast as she leaned forward. "Got things to tell you," he said.

"Later," Alberta breathed. "God, I've been on fire ever since you left."

"Then the volunteer fire department is at your service, honey," he said, and Alberta's hand reached out, rested on his chest, moved down along his body, and her touch coursed through him. She pushed her hand slowly down over his abdomen, onto the dark nap of hair below it, and he heard her gasp as she closed her fingers around him. He felt his body answer her touch with eager response and she gasped again as he grew under her grasp, pressing her fingers apart.

"God, oh, God," Alberta breathed, and he half-turned, pushed the dressing gown from her, and she sat straight as it fell away, her long breasts swaying gently. He leaned forward, took one full bottom into his mouth, and she cried out as her hand began to stroke, pull, press, and he felt her bring her legs around to cover his. She moved, rubbed her pubic mound over him, up and down, and he felt the little fleshy protuberance quiver. "Please, Fargo, please, quick . . . please quick," she whispered, and he smiled. There was no demand in her voice, no more playing the game of authority. He turned, still with her breast in his mouth, and she cried out in pleasure-pain that turned to eager desire as he slid slowly into her.

Alberta's long figure drew in, then pushed upward with him as she went into a sinuous, horizontal dance. "Aaaah, aaah, ah, ah, ah," her gasps came, slow and long first, then in quick succession. Her voice rose, became a cry, a moan, a wail, changing tone with his every movement, and her long legs came against him, the thin extra layer of flesh on them quivering around his sides. He felt her climaxing, the long body pushing upward with added vigor and her cries growing suddenly hoarse, almost breathless sounds until she suddenly burst out words. "Now, now, come . . . come . . . with me, with me, oh, God . . . iiiiieee . . ." The words turned to a cry again and the cry trailing off into that exploding moment as she clutched arms and legs tight, held herself in space as her warm funnel vibrated around him. Finally, a groaned sigh escaping her parted lips, she fell back and he stayed with her, his mouth pulling gently on one brownish nipple. "Jesus," Alberta breathed. "Oh, Jesus."

He stayed with her until he felt her go completely limp, then he slid from her to lay beside her, taking in the long breasts that fell halfway down from her chest to touch against his skin. She lay gathering breath back and finally half-turned, pushed onto one elbow, and the lavender eyes were still half-veiled as she met his gaze. "You had something to tell me," Alberta remarked.

"You're going to need a new foreman," Fargo said blandly and saw the half-veil disappear from her eyes. She frowned at him in silent waiting, and he told her about Yakes and the Sioux. He told her the core of it, but he left out Janet's presence. Unformed reasons, nagging uncertainties pushed at him, and he stayed silent about Janet. Besides, the night wasn't over and he saw no point in possibly ruining the rest of it. "Seth Bailey did a fine job of filling in for Yakes," he said.

"You'd do a better one," she answered, and her arms slid around his neck and she pressed the full bottoms of the long breasts into his chest. "Stay, take over, Fargo. We'd make a great pair," she said.

"I'm a trailsman, not a cowpuncher," he told her.

"You could be both," she said. "Work with me here. There's a lot of money to be made here at the Double-C." He started to answer but she put her fingers over his mouth. "Think about it," she said. "I have to go town in the morning and proper manners says you should tell Abram about the drive. We can talk more when I get back."

He nodded agreement. The morning, when he'd be dressed and ready to ride, would be a better time for refusing. Besides, it wasn't the time for talking. He reached down and let his hand find the warm moistness between her thighs.

"God, yes," Alberta cried out as her legs fell open. He caressed, touched, stroked, and listened to her cries spiral into the air until she tugged at him with frantic desire and he came to her again as the room echoed with the sounds of her ecstasy once more.

When she lay with satiated heaviness beside him, he felt her hand come to rest over his still-large maleness until there was only the stillness of sweet afterglow and finally Alberta rose from the bed. "I'd best get back. Abram's been restless lately," she said. "And I've things to tend to in the morning in town."

"Think I'll sleep late," Fargo told her.

"We'll talk when I get back tomorrow," Alberta said, and the air of authority had come into her voice again.

Fargo smiled as she slipped the dressing gown on and disappeared from the room. He turned on his side and slept almost at once, only to wake as he heard the sound of horses outside. He rose, went to the window, and saw the two men helping Owen Farrow from his horse. They stepped back and Owen managed to stay on his feet as he staggered drunkenly to the house, fell against the door, rested a moment, and stumbled inside. Fargo heard the two men laugh as they rode away and he returned to the bed, frowning. He closed his eyes again and it took only a few moments longer for him to sleep as he stretched out and enjoyed the luxury of the soft bed.

It was midmorning when he woke and he gazed out the window to see the day was dark, heavy grayness hanging in the sky. The ranch was quiet, only the few hands that stayed seeing to the young stock in the corrals. He washed and dressed and went to the kitchen, where he found the coffeepot on the fire. He wandered into the living room with the mug in hand and he found Abram Farrow in one of the stuffed chairs. "Alberta told me you'd come back," Abram said. "Everything go well?"

"Almost," Fargo said, and told Abram about the drive and the incident with Yakes. Abram Farrow's tired face grimaced when he finished. "Too bad," the man muttered. "Alberta always had more confidence in Yakes than I did. But I'm glad there was no more trouble. How was Dodge City?"

"Crowded, busy, lots of buyers," Fargo said.

Abram pulled a roll of bills from his pocket and pushed it at Fargo. "Balance of your pay. Extra two hundred there," he said. "Alberta said you earned it."

"Much obliged," Fargo said as his eyes narrowed. Alberta clearly had held back the real reason for the extra money. She'd concocted the need for the payroll, it had become clear. Why? he asked himself. Had Janet been right, after all? The question stabbed at him even as he knew he didn't really want to find the answer. He wanted only to be on his way, he decided again.

"We're real shorthanded till the rest of the men get back," he heard Abram Farrow say. "I'd pay you well to stay on for another week."

Fargo smiled inwardly as Alberta's wishes came out of Abram Farrow's mouth. "Don't think I can do that," Fargo said.

"Think on it," the man said, and Fargo rose and returned the coffee mug to the kitchen. He went outside instead of returning to the living room and walked to the stable, checked the Ovaro's hooves, and ran expert hands over the horse. The pinto was in fine shape, he saw happily, no foot troubles and no signs of still-fatigued muscles. He'd just finished when Alberta rode up, her horse lathered. Her eyes found him at once. She dismounted and marched toward him with fury in her face.

"Janet has those two young calves she ordered back here," she spit at him. "Herb Owler told me she bought some of his special feed this morning. Damn you, Fargo, you helped her get them back. She couldn't have done it this fast otherwise."

"I helped her," he admitted calmly. "Didn't see anything wrong in it."

"You lied to me," Alberta blazed.

"Didn't lie, just didn't mention it. Seemed no reason to. It didn't slow down your getting the payroll. Or maybe that never meant a damn thing," Fargo said.

"What do you mean?" Alberta asked, her eyes narrowing.

"Maybe you hired me just so's Janet wouldn't do so," he accused.

"No, no, of course not," Alberta said quickly, the denial perhaps too quick, Fargo reflected.

"Why'd you give Abram a cock-and-bull story about the two hundred dollars?" he pressed. "Because you didn't really need that payroll back?"

He saw her lips tighten for an instant as thoughts raced behind the lavender eyes. "Because I didn't want him to know I gave you extra money to bring you back to me in a hurry," she said. "He's always suspicious, anyway. That's why I did it, really, to bring you back to me right away."

Her voice had grown soft, almost breaking. She could think fast, he knew. Maybe there was truth in the answer. Maybe it was all true, and maybe none of it was. She'd certainly been hot for him last night. There'd been no deceit there. He swore inwardly. She's come up with answers he couldn't entirely reject. But he wouldn't swallow them whole-hog, either, he decided. "No matter." He shrugged. "I'm going to be heading out."

"No," she said quickly. "Not yet. I want you to think some more about staying on. Besides, it's going to snow. You don't want to head out in a snowstorm."

His glance went to the sky and he grunted wryly. Almost as if she'd ordered it, he saw the snow clouds hanging and felt the sharp stab of the wind. Riding out into the season's first storm didn't appeal, he admitted to himself.

"Stay here tonight. Think some more, relax," Alberta said, and dropped her voice to a half-whisper. "I lied to bring you hurrying back to me. I just told you that. Stay, please."

"Maybe," he allowed.

"I'll come to you if I can, promise," she said, and walked back to her horse.

"Going someplace?" he asked.

"To town. I have to order supplies, mostly household things," Alberta answered.

"Didn't you just come back from town?" Fargo asked mildly.

"No, no, I was tending to some other things," Alberta said, almost stumbling over words. She sent the horse into a canter and hurried away and he watched her ride from the ranch, his eyes narrowing. She was hiding something. She'd told him last night she had to go to town first thing in the morning. She'd just come back from someplace. He turned and pulled himself onto the Ovaro. He rode from the ranch and stayed back far enough not to be seen, her trail fresh and easy to follow.

He'd ridden a little more than a half-hour and saw the trail did indeed lead toward Rock Hollow and he increased his pace until he reached town. The trail ran into Main Street and he swerved the Ovaro behind a row of frame buildings as he rode forward, slowing to peer out between each.

He'd reached the last structure when he spotted her, still on her horse and halted off to one side of the street. Leaning forward intently in the saddle, she spoke to three men. Fargo held the Ovaro close against the building wall as he took in the three men. Drifters, he figured, cracked leather, worn clothes, and stained hats, men with backyard hound eyes.

Fargo watched as they nodded at Alberta's words and he edged his horse backward until he reached the rear of the building. He turned and slowly rode from town along the back edge of the town buildings and quickened his pace when he left Rock Hollow. He frowned as he rode; Alberta had lied to him and tried to cover it up by admitting the fact but giving an emotional reason. Had she been using the technique of admitting a small lie to cover up something bigger?

He returned to the Farrow ranch with a sour taste in his mouth, tethered his horse, and went into the house, where he found Owen Farrow clutching a cup of coffee. Fargo stared at the youth. Owen's reddened eyes seemed even more red against the pastiness of his drawn face and the cup shook in his hand. Night after night of heavy drinking had caught up with the resiliency of youth.

"Heard you were back," Owen muttered as he sipped his coffee.

"Came back with your sister," Fargo said casually.

Owen Farrow frowned in surprise at him. "Janet's back already?"

"With her two new calves," Fargo said blandly, and saw the younger man stare at him with openmouthed astonishment.

Owen Farrow finally pulled his jaw shut, pushed himself to his feet, and head down, hurried from the room. Fargo watched him go down the hallway to a room at the far end of the hall and pull the door shut behind him, clearly upset. The Trailsman's lips were pursed in thought as he stepped outside. He'd seen more than surprise in Owen Farrow's reaction. His eyes had held almost panic, certainly anger and fear. First Alberta and now Owen, and Fargo had to wonder once again if Barnaby Tilden had told the truth about his three missing men. He started to turn back into the house when he felt the harsh blast of wind and wetness hit the back of his neck. Snow was swirling downward, suddenly thick, blotting out the sky. He halted, his eyes moving across the buildings and corrals taking in a mantle of white before he turned away and walked to the guest room.

The snow and the hour had darkened the last of the day and he turned the lamp on low as he stretched across the bed. The snow was a driving white curtain outside the window. No flurries now, but a full blown winter storm. Fargo lay back and felt uneasiness pull at him as he wondered about Janet and Bunker Bixby.

When he heard Alberta's voice from down the hall, he grunted. Both she and Owen were at the ranch, but that didn't reassure him and he had to force himself to wait in the room as night fell and the snow blanketed the window. He had already decided against confronting Alberta. He'd try to draw her out first, perhaps let her trap herself. He'd use the bed to open her up in more ways than one.

But another hour passed before he heard the door open and he rose as Alberta came in. "I can't get away yet. Abram wants to go over bills. I'll come after he goes to sleep," she said. "You just wait right here." She tossed him a quick smile and spun from the room to pull the door closed after her.

Fargo muttered an oath as the uneasiness speared at him again. He'd no reason to disbelieve her, but he couldn't believe her about anything now. He went to the window, but the swirling snow let him see only a white curtain and he turned away, his hands clenched. He forced himself to stretch out on the bed again and listen to the wind blow outside. He rose a dozen times to pace the small room and was on the edge of the bed when Alberta finally returned. She took only a few steps into the room. "He's still awake. He wants me to stay with him," she said. "I'll come back later if I can. You know I'll try."

"I know I'm not much for waiting," Fargo growled.

"Get some rest, I know you can use it," Alberta said. "I'll be back if I can. Just wait for me." She blew a kiss at him and backed from the room with a quick half-step.

Fargo frowned at the door that closed after her. She was stringing him along. She wanted him here, waiting the night through, and he pulled the door open, paused until she was down the hall, and strode quickly to the other wing of the house. His uneasiness had suddenly become a gnawing pain, and he went to the room Owen Farrow had entered earlier. He knocked, waited, knocked again. No one answered and he closed one big hand over the doorknob and twisted. The door came open, the room empty. He cursed silently and hurried to the living room, then the kitchen. The house was silent, Owen Farrow no place about.

Fargo took three long strides to reach the front door and plunged out into the swirling snow. A light glowed as a faint yellow smear through the snow from the bunkhouse and he bent his head as he made his way toward it. He reached the bunkhouse and pushed the door open to enter with a flurry of snow trailing after him. The four cowhands there looked up as he halted. "Been trying to find Owen," Fargo said. "Anybody here seen him?"

"He rode out," one man said.

"When?" Fargo asked.

"Earlier this afternoon, maybe three, four hours back," the man answered.

"Obliged," Fargo said, hurried back into the snow, and he let the curse fall from his lips. "Goddamn," he swore as he made his way to the Ovaro and pulled his sheepskin coat from the saddlebag. Owen Farrow had deliberately gone into his room, waited, slipped out when he saw the chance. Fargo felt the gnawing inside his stomach turn to cold apprehension, and his heavy winter jacket on, he climbed onto the Ovaro and rode from the ranch. The ground was deeply blanketed in snow and he knew the storm could easily disorient the average man until he was hopelessly lost in a white, trackless void. But the Trailsman called upon the instincts and the knowledge that made him what he was. He first used the outline of the ranch to determine the way he wanted to go, northwest, and he paused to feel where the wind blew against his face. The sharp wind blew hardest against the right side of his face, he noted, and he sent the Ovaro forward.

Even with his head bent low against the storm, he could feel the wind and he held the horse on a steady northwest track as he used his face and the wind as a natural compass. He corrected direction whenever he felt the wind at his face from another angle, and he moved forward through the storm, adjusting, shifting, correcting whenever the wind told him he'd drifted from his course. He let the Ovaro set his own pace, the snow soft and heavy, and he felt the icy sharpness of the cold, which not even the thick coat could entirely shut out. He felt the horse pull up a low hill, then another, and he cursed the slowness of his progress, but he was finally nearing Janet's place and he corrected his course again as the wind changed against his face. He'd ridden down a slight incline and he strained his eyes as he peered through the snowfall when suddenly he saw the flakes lessen, the white curtain shred as with its own unaccountableness the storm halted. He drove the Ovaro forward and glimpsed Janet's neat log and frame house with the stable attached.

He rode closer and felt the cold apprehension inside himself becoming a rock in the pit of his stomach. The door of the stable hung open, the flickering of lamplight reaching out from the front door of the house. He reined up, leapt down to the ground, and landed halfway up to his calves in the snow. He ran, pulled the door open, and felt his lips pull back as he saw the chairs upended, the small table on its side, and against the bed, Bunker Bixby leaning back, one hand to the red stain that ran from his rib cage to his hip. The old man opened his eyes as Fargo dropped to one knee beside him. "Can you talk?" he asked, and saw that a sheet had been torn and strapped around Bunker Bixby's left side. The old man nodded and Fargo helped him sit straighter. "What happened?" he questioned.

"They rushed in, shooting. We never heard 'em come," Bunker rasped. "They got me with the first shot."

"Janet?" Fargo asked.

"I saw one hit her with his pistol and she went down," the old man said. "I lay still and they thought I was dead."

"They just up and left?" Fargo frowned.

"No, I heard them go into the stable and take the calves," Bunker said. "I crawled to the door as they took off. I winged one of them coming through the trees, heard him yell and saw him grab at his shoulder. But he kept going."

"Where's Janet?"

"She came to and saw to me first. When I told her I could hold out she went out to look for the calves. She figured they'd be going to drop them in the storm to freeze to death," Bunker said. "I told her she'd only get herself frozen to death out there, but she rushed out."

"Can you still hold out?" Fargo asked, and Bunker nodded.

"So long as I don't have to do anything but lay here," he said.

"I'll be back for you," Fargo told him as he ran from the door. The stillness of the snow-covered night wrapped itself around him and he peered at the tracks still visible in the snow. The attackers had come from the left side and ridden off the same way, then turned and went north. He walked a few yards farther and saw the blood spots in the snow, in the trees, apart from the other tracks. Then he found what he sought, the single prints of Janet's roan as she'd ridden off north, and he swung onto the Ovaro and followed the trail. The new snow hadn't had time to erase her tracks before the storm ended and he suddenly veered away to ride east, where he picked up the tracks of two horses. Janet had stayed north and he followed the trail in the snow to a cluster of cedars where the tracks turned sharply to go south.

He halted, let the Ovaro blow air through his nostrils, and rubbed his hand down the horses's smooth neck to quiet him. He sat motionless in the stillness and suddenly he heard it, the faint bleat in the silence. He turned the Ovaro along the edge of the cedars and spotted the small gray-white form almost covered by the snow. He reined to a halt, dismounted, and picked the calf out of the deadly white blanket. He slung the calf over the front of the saddle, pulled himself back onto the Ovaro, and turned west until he picked up Janet's tracks again. She'd continued on, following another pair of tracks, and he pressed forward, partly covering the calf with the bottom of his coat.

He spied her finally, a dark form against the gray-white expanse of the snow-covered terrain, and he heard the sound of the calf. She was still trying to get the little Charolais up onto the roan when he reached her.

"Oh, God, oh, thank God, Fargo," Janet breathed as he swung down and boosted the second calf onto the roan. Janet fell against him, clung there for a moment, then pulled back, her eyes on the calf across his saddle. "Thank you, oh, God, thank you," she said. "There's one more."

"We'll look as we go back," he said. "We'd better get these two warm or you'll lose them, too."

She nodded agreement and swung onto the roan to follow him as he headed back. His eyes swept the snow as they rode and the moon peeked through low, scudding clouds to touch the land with ghostly brilliance, but he saw no sign of the third calf and he finally slowed as they reached the neat house. He took the two young calves into the house and laid them before the fireplace as Janet rushed to Bunker. "It's still bleeding too much. We've got to get him to Doc Teller in town," he heard her say as he built up the fire.

"Get blankets while I hitch up the wagon," he said, and hurried out to the stable. When he drove the deep cotton-bed wagon outside, Janet was ready with blankets. He went into the house, left the calves warming beside the fire, and carried Bunker Bixby to the wagon

Janet saw that Bunker lay as comfortable as possible and heaped blankets on him before she climbed onto the seat beside Fargo.

"This wagon is coming in mighty handy," she said as she pulled her coat tighter. "You just going to write off the other calf?"

"Two's better than none," he said, and she understood in silence.

"What made you come?" she asked quietly.

"A gut feeling. Too many things I didn't like and nothing I can prove," he said. "But I was right. Somebody came after you."

"Barnaby Tilden," Janet snapped. She waited through his silence. "He has the men for it. Why can't you see that?"

"Men can be hired," he muttered. "By anybody."

"If you're talking about Owen again, I don't believe it," Janet said. "He's my brother."

"So he is," Fargo commented.

"You said you've no proof of anything," she returned.

"You've no proof about Barnaby Tilden either," he reminded her.

She took the answer in silence, said nothing more till the wagon rolled into the darkened streets of Rock Hollow. "First house on the left," she said, and he drew to a halt before a modest sign that proclaimed: DOC JOSEPH TELLER. Janet hopped from the wagon to pound on the door where a light shone over the transom as Fargo pulled the tailgate of the wagon down and lifted Bunker out. The doctor, dressed and wearing a white coat, held the door open wide as Fargo carried Bunker into the house and put him on a wooden pallet in the first room.

The doctor, his short white coat hanging loosely over a spare, thin frame, lifted spectacles from his pocket and put them on as he cut away the makeshift bandages. A middle-aged woman with graying hair held in a bun appeared with a basin of hot water and rolls of bandages, her body as plump as Doc Teller's was thin.

"He's lost a fair amount of blood and he's got two splintered ribs," the doctor said as he examined Bunker. "But we won't have to go digging around for a bullet. It passed through his rib cage. Rest and medicine for a few weeks ought to pull him through." He helped the woman apply fresh bandages and clean the wound and he straightened up slowly when he finished. "We'll keep him for a week. You can take him home then," he said to Janet.

"Whatever you say, Doc," she agreed.

"Busy night, considering the storm, especially," the doctor said. "Second gunshot case in the past few hours."

Fargo felt Janet stiffen. "Who was the other one?" he asked.

"One of Barnaby Tilden's hands, shot in the shoulder," the doctor said, and Fargo cast a glance at Janet. Her face had grown tight and she whirled and strode from the house.

"Thanks, Doc," Fargo said, and followed her outside to find her on the wagon, the reins in hand, her lips a thin line.

"Heard enough?" she hissed as he climbed onto the seat beside her. She snapped the reins and sent the horses into a gallop. Fargo stared into the night with brows drawn as Janet sent the heavy wagon spraying snow. He sat in silence and felt the waves of fury from her. Anger stabbed at him also as he sent his own thoughts racing, quickly pulling together everything that he'd filed away in his mind, and when Janet skidded the Owensboro to a halt in front of her place, he'd sorted out enough to know that the truth still lay hidden.

"I'll put the wagon away," he said, and Janet tossed him the reins as she leapt down and ran into the house. He moved the wagon into the stable, unhitched the horses, and returned to the house.

She was in the center of the room, loading a big, old Hawken plains rifle with a cartridge pouch on the chair beside her.

"What do you think you're going to do?" he asked.

"Give Barnaby Tilden some of his own medicine," she said as she finished loading the rifle.

"You mean get yourself killed," he said.

"I'll be just fine," she snapped.

"Put that rifle down. You're back to jumping to conclusions again," he said.

Janet stared incredulously at him. "Bixby winged one of them in the shoulder. What more do you want?" she shouted.

"Proof," he said.

"What's wrong with you? Why can't you see it was Tilden?" she demanded.

"Maybe it was, but I want a chance to be sure," Fargo said.

"I'm sure, now," Janet snapped.

"You were sure I was a damn coward," he said, and saw her lips tighten.

"One for you," she glowered.

"If it's Tilden, I'll help you get him," he said, and she stared at him, her round face glowering.

"Promise?" she asked.

"My word," he told her. She lowered the rifle and he reached out and took it from her. He set it in a corner of the room as her eyes followed him.

"Why do you keep backing away from admitting it's Barnaby Tilden?" she asked, more curiosity than fury in her voice now.

"Little things that don't prove out but don't fit right either," he told her as he went to the calves and ran his hands over them. "They're warmed through. I'll put them back in their stall now," he said. She produced a length of clothesline and he fashioned it into two halters and led the calves from the house, went over them once more when he had them in the stable, and was satisfied they'd come through without any real harm.

Janet had straightened the house some, cleaned away blood spots where Bunker had lain, and faced him as he entered. "Stay the night?" she asked. "What if they come back?

"They won't. They figure they've done in the calves," Fargo said.

"Alberta waiting for you?" Janet asked waspishly.

"Maybe, but not the way you mean." He laughed.

"She's not waiting with another bedroom reward?" Janet slid out.

"Not tonight," he answered, and let a touch of rue enter his voice. Her eyes flared instantly and he smiled inwardly. He turned her invitation in his mind and thought of Alberta's rage when she found her little game hadn't worked and he hadn't stayed safely under her thumb. He'd let her pace the night away, he decided, certain that her nerves were already rubbed raw by now. Janet's voice, laced with disdain, out into his thoughts.

"I'm so sorry for you," she said stiffly. "But you're welcome to stay anyway."

"Think I will," he said. "I'll just stretch out here by the fire, unless you've a better offer."

"I do not," she flared. "I'm no stand-in, I'll have you know," she said, and he caught the hurt inside the anger.

"I know that," he said gently, put a finger under her chin, and lifted her pugnacious little face up. "I didn't mean it that way," he said, and brought his mouth to hers, softly, gently, and her lips parted just a fraction and he tasted the sweetness of her. The hazel eyes stared gravely up at him as he pulled back.

"What was that for?" she murmured.

"Apology," he said. "Always like to seal an apology."

Her face stayed grave. "Seal it again," she said.

He brought his mouth to her, remained gentle, and felt the softness of her full lips part a little further. He let the tip of his tongue slide forward, flick across her lips, and he felt her flinch, then press against him, her lips opening wider, growing firm as she kissed him back, but then she twisted away. "I can't, not now," she said. "I keep thinking about you with Alberta. Maybe, when it's all over," she said.

He said nothing but rubbed his hand along the back of her neck, moving lightly down along the soft skin at the top of her back and shoulders. She didn't move but her breath drew in sharply and the round, high breasts lifted. "Damn you," she said as she spun away from him, ran into the next room, and pulled the door shut.

He laughed softly as he shed his clothes and lay down before the fire on a sheet she had left on a chair. His face slowly hardened as his thoughts turned from Janet. Come dawn, he'd have a one-sided talk with Barnaby Tilden. He couldn't dismiss Tilden, especially not after tonight. If he wore two faces, maybe this was just one more example of it, Fargo pondered. But even so, there were too many things that still refused to fit.

He pushed away further speculation and swore at

Janet under his breath. From that very first day she'd drawn him into it and now he'd let himself be pulled in further. Hell, there was no point in backing off now, he told himself. He closed his eyes certain of only one thing: Barnaby Tilden wouldn't be the only one answering questions, and as it usually happened, truth would hide in the unsaid more than the said.

6

Morning dawned sharp, cold, and bright, and Fargo dressed quickly before he paused at the door to the other room. He heard no sounds and pressed carefully against the door until it opened enough for him to see into the room. Janet lay still asleep on a wide cot, a quilt over her that had slipped off at one side, and he saw a firm, tanned leg that curved smoothly upward to disappear exasperatingly under the cover at the line of her hip. She turned on her side, and her round-cheeked face, like a little girl's, stayed half under the quilt. He backed silently from the door and made his way outside to the stable. She was still asleep, he was sure, when he rode the Ovaro in the early-day sun.

He made tracks through the snow, now hardened into firmness that made better footing for the horse, guiding the Ovaro toward Barnaby Tilden's spread. He reached the knot of buckeyes and steered the horse into the trees until, at the other end, he dismounted and pulled the big Sharps from its saddle holster.

Tilden's ranch was just coming to life, he saw as he crawled a half-dozen yards from the trees to a fair-sized rock and positioned himself against it. The big rifle raised atop the rock, the stock against his shoulder, he watched five of Tilden's hands begin their chores at the corrals. He continued to peer down the rifle barrel at the main house and his eyes narrowed when he saw the front door open. Tilden came out, his red vest on, another man walking beside him. Tilden walked from the house to the first line of fence posts while the other man continued on toward the barn.

Fargo squinted as he took aim, waited until Barnaby Tilden came to a halt and rested one foot on the bottom rail of the fence. He squeezed the trigger and the big Sharps resounded in the morning stillness. Tilden's hat flew from his head and the man dived for the ground, to lay there for a moment, his six-gun in his hand. Fargo fired two more shots, bracketing Tilden with them as the man rolled, then rolled back again.

"Don't move, Tilden," Fargo called. He saw the hands rushing from the corrals and the bunkhouse. "Tell your boys to stay back or I'll blow your head off," Fargo said. For emphasis, he fired a shot that slammed into the ground a fraction of an inch from the man's face.

Tilden jumped back as he called to his men. "Stay there . . . don't do anything dumb," the man ordered.

"Very good," Fargo said.

"You bastard, I'll kill you for this," Tilden swore.

"You've got it backward, mister. You give me answers or you're dead," Fargo said. To affirm his words, he fired another bracket of shots. One sent up a spray of dirt an inch from Tilden's shoulder, the other whistling across the top of his head so close that his hair blew.

"Jesus," Tilden gasped.

"You've got the idea," Fargo said. "Now, sit up." He watched the man gingerly push himself to a sitting position.

"You're crazy, Fargo, you know that," the man said.

"You raided Janet Farrow's place last night," Fargo said.

"Hell I did," Barnaby Tilden bristled.

"One of your men was shot. The doc treated him. Don't try to hogwash me. If I get upset, I could miss missing," Fargo said.

"Now, hold on, I can explain that," Tilden said hastily.

"I want to hear that," Fargo returned.

"We lost a half-dozen yearlings. Three of my boys were out trying to find them when the storm blew up. They kept looking and they were near Janet's place. They heard the shooting and went down to see if there was any trouble. Tim Hansen got there first. He was still moving through the trees when the shot blasted him from the cabin and he hightailed it out of there," Tilden said. "That's the damn truth, Fargo."

"It's real neat, too, isn't it?" Fargo said.

"It's still the truth, goddammit," Tilden shouted.

"I'll find out. If you're lying, I'll be coming back, and when I do, you'll pay for it," Fargo said. "Now lay down again and close your eyes." Tilden swore half under his breath as he obeyed. "Now, you or any of your boys do anything stupid and you're a dead man," Fargo said. "You hear me, Tilden?"

"I hear you," the man said, his voice muffled into the grass.

Fargo rose to a crouch and backed from the rock, his

eyes sweeping the figures against the corral. They stayed frozen in place and he backed to the buckeyes, swung onto the Ovaro, and cantered away through the trees. He rode with thoughts racing, turning Barnaby Tilden's words in his mind. He had started toward the Farrow ranch when he changed directions and rode into Rock Hollow to halt at the doctor's house. The ample-figured woman opened the door and he glimpsed Doc Teller with a cup of coffee in hand.

"He's doing well," the doctor said. "He's a tough old bird."

"Can I talk to him a minute?" Fargo asked, and the doctor nodded. Bunker was awake, Fargo saw as he entered the room, his shock of white hair looking even whiter somehow.

"Janet all right?" the old man asked, and Fargo heard the weakness in his voice.

"She's holding up," Fargo said. "Answer me something. That figure you winged last night, I found the bloodstains in the trees apart from the other tracks. Did you see him with the others that hightailed it with the calves?"

Bunker thought for a moment. "Can't say I did," he answered. "They were on their way when I crawled to the door. I just saw a shape through the snow and fired. I figured he was with the others."

"Maybe he was," Fargo said. "I just wanted to pin down that much. You stay quiet and do what the doc tells you." He rose and hurried from the house, and this time he headed the Ovaro for the Farrow ranch. It was near noon when he rode in and he saw Alberta in the doorway, fire in the lavender eyes.

"You bastard," she hissed as he dismounted and reached the doorway.

His smile was affable. "Got tired of waiting," he said.

"I told you I'd be back," she said.

"So's I'd stay there for the night," Fargo said. "It didn't work."

Alberta's eyes grew smaller. "What does that mean?" she asked.

"We'll make it a game. I'll answer your questions and you'll answer mine," he said, his voice turning sharp.

"What questions?" Alberta asked warily.

"That little conference you had in town yesterday morning. What was it all about?" he tossed at her, and saw the surprise flood into her eyes.

"You've been busy," she said icily.

"You, too, honey," he growled.

"I don't have to tell you my business," Alberta said stiffly.

"Not unless you want me to haul your ass in for attempted murder and cattle theft," he answered. "Hired guns hit Janet's place last night, maybe the ones you were so busy giving orders yesterday." Alberta's eyes speared into him. "I could start by telling Abram what happened and what I saw. Then I could tell the sheriff," Fargo said, knowing the first threat would carry more weight than the second.

She turned away for a moment, stepped into the hall, and he followed. "I had hired those men to stop her from bringing the two calves back. I'll admit that. I hired them to intercept her and take the calves," Alberta said. "But I didn't expect she'd be doing that for at least another week or two. When I found out you'd already brought the calves back with her, I had to go to town, find them, and call everything off. I had to pay them for waiting around, too. That's what I was doing when you saw me."

"Is it?" he pressed. "Or were you just changing their orders?"

"No," Alberta said sharply. "I paid them and called it off."

"Got anything besides words to prove it?" Fargo asked.

"No," she said.

"Not enough," he bit out, and turned from her.

"What are you going to do?" she called after him as he started to walk from her, fear in her voice.

"Think," he said. "Where's Owen?"

"He took a mug of coffee into his room," Alberta said, and stepped forward to press her hand into his forearm. "I did come back last night, to stay the rest of the night," she said. "Believe me, Fargo. Don't do anything foolish. We can do so much here together. Give me another chance."

"Sure." He smiled. "Everybody's going to get another chance."

"What's that mean?" She frowned.

He shrugged. "Another chance at the truth," he said, and strode down the hall to the room at the far end. His knock on the door was sharp and the face that opened it seemed twenty years older than it was. Drawn, dark circles hung from Owen Farrow's reddened eyes and his skin hung loosely. Fargo's eyes were ice-blue as he stepped into the room. "You sneaked away yesterday. Why?" Fargo snapped.

The youth tried to muster indignation. "Didn't sneak away. Just went out, that's all," he said.

"Where?" Fargo growled.

"None of your damn business." Owen Farrow frowned.

The big man's hand shot out, closed around the front of Owen Farrow's shirt, and lifted the youth off the ground. "You've two seconds to answer me or I put your head through the wall, junior," Fargo said.

"To town, to the Silver Garter," Owen Farrow croaked. Fargo let him drop and Owen Farrow rubbed his throat with one hand. "Hired guns hit Janet's place last night. Took the calves," Fargo said. "You wouldn't know anything about it, would you?"

The youth slumped into a chair. "No," he muttered. He cocked a glance at the big man towering over him. "She's all right, isn't she?" he asked nervously.

"Just a bump on her head," Fargo said. "You can prove you were at the Silver Garter, I take it."

"Sure. Played poker all night. Ed Carver will tell you that," Owen Farrow said. He stared into space for a moment, let his glance slide to the big man. "It's over then, now," he went on. "She's lost the calves. She can't get any more till spring. Maybe she'll give it up. Maybe it's all for the best this way, for Janet and for everybody else."

"Maybe," Fargo said. "I'll tell her that." He pulled the door open, left the house, and returned to the Ovaro, which was tethered outside. He glimpsed Alberta at a window watching him ride away, her face tight. Everyone had a neat, pat explanation, he mused as he rode toward Rock Hollow once more. Only, someone was lying. Barnaby Tilden? he wondered. Did he really wear two faces, one kind, the other ruthless? Or did Alberta's steely determination to protect her interest lead her to stop at nothing? And there was Owen Farrow, desperately afraid of anything that threatened his pot of gold. He was weak, yet even the weak fought out of desperation with their own twisted brand of venomousness. Fargo turned the sorry thoughts over again. He was close to the truth of the matter, but he needed those last pieces that would make things fall into place.

He shut off further speculation as he reached town and drew to a halt outside the Silver Garter. The place was not filled as it was by night, but there were customers on hand and he glimpsed three men disappear behind the curtain to the gaming tables. His glance found the dapper, diminutive figure atop the raised platform that let him survey the floor. Ed Carver, the diamond stickpin in his cravat sparkling, watched the big man come toward him.

"Been wondering when you'd stop by again," the little man said. "Heard you and Barnaby Tilden had words."

"You could say that." Fargo smiled. "Came to ask something. Owen Farrow, was he here last night?"

"He was," Ed Carver said, and Fargo saw the man's darting eyes grow cautious.

"He lose at poker again?" Fargo questioned.

Ed Carver's smile was careful. "Owen's not a very good card player, but he won't admit it," the man said.

"I've seen your boys bring him home," Fargo remarked.

"A courtesy to our customers," the little man said.

"How much will you let a man lose?" Fargo asked casually, but saw Ed Carver's little eyes grow careful.

"We don't have any limits on winning or losing," the man answered.

"How much is Owen Farrow into you for?" Fargo asked with sudden sharpness.

"We don't talk about our customers, Fargo," Ed Carver said evenly.

"Too bad." Fargo smiled. "Be seeing you." The dapper little man nodded but his darting eyes were veiled. Fargo sauntered from the saloon, a grim smile edging his lips. He rode from town as the afternoon shadows lengthened. A half-mile from town he steered the horse into a thicket of alders and slid from the saddle. He rested, half-dozing against a tree trunk as night fell and the cold's icy fingers clutched at him. He finally climbed into the saddle again and set off on the road leading to town. Few riders passed, a handful leaving town and a haywagon rolling across the road. He waited patiently and finally saw a lone horseman moving down the road at a slow trot. The moonlight touched Owen Farrow's drawn face as he rode by, and Fargo watched him go toward town until he was out of sight. He rode out of the alders and sent the Ovaro into a fast trot that took him north past the Farrow ranch until he saw the neat house.

When she heard the horse approaching, Janet appeared at the door, the big Hawken in hand. She lowered the rifle as the Ovaro came into sight. "Why'd you run out this morning?" She frowned as Fargo entered the house. "I wondered if you were coming back."

"I'm here," he said. "Hungry, too."

"I've rabbit stew on. It's about ready," she said. "What did you find out?"

"Had a talk with Tilden, not that he enjoyed it too much." Fargo smiled and sat down. He told her what Tilden had said to explain the wounded man, and Janet frowned at him when he finished. Her round, high breasts were pressed tight against a gray shirt as she stood with hands on her hips.

"He lied, of course, made it up. Are you going to tell me you believe him?" she accused.

"I believe myself," Fargo said calmly. "The blood on the snow was not with the other tracks, didn't follow after them. It just could be Tilden's telling the truth."

"You're impossible. I don't understand you," Janet

flared, and stirred the stew pot with such vigor the contents sloshed over the edge.

"You've said that before," he remarked.

She shot a sharp glance at him. "It's not just the bloodstains, is it?" she said. "You've never believed Barnaby Tilden's the one. You've other reasons."

"Maybe," he agreed. "Let's eat and I'll tell you some of it."

"Why only some of it?" Janet asked as she put out tin plates and began to dish the stew.

"I won't talk about what I'm not sure of yet, but I'll tell you the rest," he said. "I guess it's time for that. Tilden's not the only one with reasons, though he has good ones, I'll admit that." Janet listened soberly as he told her what he'd learned about Alberta and what she'd admitted to him. He told her next of Owen's gambling and drinking and how Owen, too, had disappeared the night before. When he finished, she stared in silence at him for a long minute. "Not Owen," she said. "He was gambling, Ed Carver backed him up on that. He wouldn't hire anyone to hurt me. Owen's always been weak, but that's all, just weak. He's not behind it. He cares too much about me. The things he said to you prove that. He was concerned about me. He wanted to know if I was all right."

"He did," Fargo agreed.

"He wants it to be over so I'll be safe," Janet said. "No, not Owen, absolutely not Owen."

"Alberta?" Fargo questioned.

Janet's round face crinkled in thought. "Maybe," she said finally. "She's selfish. She wouldn't stop at much to get her way." Janet paused, tossed a sharp glance at him. "But she explains everything away, too. Why do you believe Barnaby Tilden's neat answers and not Alberta's?" she pressed.

"Didn't say I did," Fargo answered.

"But you hang back on Tilden for some reason," Janet returned. "I still say he's the one. He's got the most to lose. Everybody knows he's a hard, cold man, and I'm nothing to him—not family, not friends, nothing. He's the one."

"Maybe," Fargo allowed, and her glare was one of exasperation. "Right now, everyone thinks all the calves are gone. I saw to that. I want to keep it that way a little longer. Don't buy any special feed, don't take them out of the stable. Tilden had a man watching you. He might still have one."

"And you still aren't sure it's him?" Janet grimaced.

"I'm slow," he tossed back with a grin, and she made a face at him. "Is there someplace else you can hole up besides here?" Fargo asked.

She frowned in thought for a moment. "There's one place, a little cabin in a ravine about two miles north of here," she said.

"That'll do fine," Fargo said.

"But it's no real secret place. Owen and I used it when we were children. It belonged to my mother. Abram knows about it, probably Alberta, too, and Owen, of course," Janet said. "If Tilden has someone watching me, he'll probably know about it too."

"That's all right," Fargo said. "So long as it's smaller than this place."

"It's just a cabin," Janet said. "I can take you there."

"When it's time," he told her as he got to his feet.

"You're not staying?" She frowned.

"I'll be back. I've got something to check out first," he said. "I could be real late. Don't wait up."

The green-flecked hazel eyes studied him. "Something tells me I should say be careful," she answered.

"Always careful." Fargo grinned as he hurried from the house. A half-moon made the layer of snow bright and he rode at a fast trot, skirted Barnaby Tilden's spread, and finally reached Rock Hollow. The town slept, but the Silver Garter still throbbed as Fargo steered the horse to the rear of the saloon. Ed Carver had an office somewhere and chances were it was in the rear of the building. Fargo spied the window, partially open, and he slowly opened it further. He'd purposely chosen this time when the saloon was still in full swing. Carver and his men were busy out front while later, when the saloon closed, they'd be alert to any sound.

He swung one long leg over the windowsill and followed with the other. He paused in a dimly lighted corridor. At the far end he saw slivers of light slipping under two closed doors, and the murmur of voices and poker chips drifted through the doors. His back against one wall, he moved along the corridor and came to a room halfway down the hall; he slipped into it and strained his eyes in the darkness. He managed to make out the dark bulk of a small wooden desk and, beside it, a cabinet. Moving to the desk, he found a lamp and turned it on low and cursed silently when he saw there was no door to close. The little room was a windowless cubicle with an armchair behind the desk, and he circled to the back of the desk and began to ease drawers open. They held only stationery, a territory map, a handful of eyeshades, and perhaps a dozen unopened card decks. Fargo turned to the wooden cabinet, pulled at the top drawer, and found it locked.

Blowing the lock open with his Colt was out of the question, and the lock resisted all his tugs. He peered closely at the top of the drawer. The lock was sturdy but the wood around it old, pitted, and cracked. He reached down to the holster around his calf and drew out the thin, double-edged throwing knife. Using the point first, he began to dig at the wood around the lock and found it gouged easily. Using mostly the tip of the blade, he continued to poke, pry, and dig into the wood, gouging out little pieces, cutting away larger ones with the razor-sharp edges of the blade whenever he could. But progress was made of nerve-wracking slowness and he felt the little trickle of perspiration run down the side of his neck. He paused as his wrist cramped, but he renewed his efforts and suddenly saw the last splinter of wood fall away from around the lock.

Carefully, he pried the lock free, put it aside, and pulled the drawer open to stare down at the long gray-green ledger. He returned the throwing knife to its calf holster and used both hands to lift the heavy ledger from the drawer to the desk, where he spread it open at once. Pages of payroll figures and other operating expenses met his eyes first, and he leafed through them impatiently. He halted as he came to the first page of names and, across from each, a row of figures, some noted as paid, others as unpaid. There was no alphabetical order to the names, but he found dates in years and months heading the pages. He started to look for current figures when he heard the door open in the corridor. A voice followed instantly and he recognized it as Ed Carver's slightly nasal sound. "Somebody's in the office. I didn't leave the lamp on," he heard the man say. "Get Charley and the others."

Fargo cursed and turned the lamp out to plunge the room into near-total darkness. He heard the doors open again and the sound of other men hurrying into the corridor. He thought for a moment of trying to take the ledger but flung aside the thought. The book was both heavy and cumbersome and he'd be lucky to get out with his life. "He's in here," Fargo heard Ed Carver hiss. "Get the bastard."

Fargo drew the big Colt .45 and crossed the little room in one long stride. If the others reached the doorway first, they'd pour lead into the little cubicle. He had to strike first, use boldness and surprise. He dropped almost to the floor, dived forward into the corridor with the Colt blazing, and he heard shouts and curses and the sound of bodies colliding, falling backward to avoid the hail of bullets. He rolled, came to his feet, and bolted down the dark corridor. Not slowing as he reached the end of it, he dived headfirst through the open window as three shots slammed into the window frame.

"Get him," he heard Ed Carver yell as he somersaulted, regained his feet, and vaulted onto the Ovaro. He yanked the horse around and dashed between two buildings before any of his pursuers could see him. He emerged onto Main Street, raced the horse along the wide street and then in between another pair of buildings again until he was galloping out of town. It had been too dark and everything had happened too fast for Ed Carver to see him, but he knew the man would make his conclusions quickly enough. Fargo's lips pulled back as he sent the Ovaro through the cold night. He'd missed getting that final answer. He'd have to get it the hard way now.

He rode down the slope to Janet's house as the moon began to slide toward the horizon and he slowed as he reached the house, his eyes sweeping the terrain. A flicker of firelight touched the window and he slid from the saddle and led the horse into the stable. After he unsaddled the Ovaro, he checked the two calves, added a

156

half-pail of feed to the bin in the small stall, and pulled the stable door closed when he left.

He entered the house and saw the figure on the blanket in front of the fire, her pert, round face outlined by the flickering flames. She sat up as he came in and the firelight touched her hazel eyes with copper glints. "I told you not to wait up," he said.

"I dozed some," she answered. "Kept waking up. Did you get your answer?"

He folded himself on the blanket beside her. "No," he said. "My luck didn't hold out."

"Now, what?" she asked.

"One trail doesn't work, you try another," he said.

"Tired?" she asked.

"Not really," he said.

"Good," Janet said as she leaned forward and pressed her mouth to his, lingered, and parted her lips so Fargo could feel her warm sweetness. He half-smiled at her when she pulled away.

"Change your mind about waiting till it's all over?" he asked.

"Yes," she answered with her hazel eyes grave. "I guess I just got tired of lying to myself."

"Wise decision," he said as he reached out and pulled her to him with one hand and shed his gun belt with the other. Her lips opened for him hungrily and he felt her tongue slide out to rub over his lips. His hand slipped down to touch one round, high breast, and Janet quivered, reached up, and tore the gray shirt open. The round breasts tumbled out, glistening smooth, perfectly rounded, full and high, proud, pert breasts that matched her face with very tiny nipples of the faintest pink set in equally tiny pink circles. He bent down, kissed one breast, then the other, and Janet's head fell back as she cried out, a little sound that was almost a laugh. "Yes, oh, please, yes," she murmured, turned her body for him as he pulled at the skirt, slid it down her legs. Her pink bloomers came off with the skirt and he took in a rounded little figure, tiny, convex tummy, and over the little pubic mound a mass of beautifully disarrayed black ringlets. Firm, smoothly youthful legs curved below the dark triangle and she lay back to enjoy his eyes on her, a slightly chunky, youthful throbbing body that fit her round-cheeked face perfectly.

He pulled off his clothes as she encircled his neck with her arms and he saw the hazel eyes glow. He kissed her hungrily. She quivered in response as his hands caressed the high, round mounds, his thumbs moving back and forth across the tiny nipples. The left one hardened first and rose a fraction, the right one following as he caressed the little pink circles around each. She murmured delight. His mouth found one round breast, felt its firmness as she gasped in pleasure. His hand explored, tracing a burning path down across the little tummy and across her hips, then circled through the dark mass of silky ringlets. Her legs stayed together as he pressed down to the damp warmth of her tightly held thighs. He reached up and touched the edge of her dark portal, pressing against the very tip of the satin-smooth lips.

Janet shuddered, her torso lifting, falling back, and he reached deeper into the dark, moist tunnel. "Oh, Fargo, oh, yes, yes . . . God, yes," he heard her cry out, a sudden half-screamed torrent of words. Her thighs opened, stretched outward, fell open wider, and he turned to let his searching, warm maleness come over her pubic mound. "Eeee . . . iiii . . . ah, ah, ah . . ." Janet half-screamed, and he felt her pelvis lift, twist, push upward, the glove seeking the hand. He felt her begin to move up and down all by herself, desire unwilling to wait, a rehearsal of the senses.

"Please, please, come . . . come to me, God, come to me," Janet murmured as she pumped her body, and he felt her throbbing urgency sweep over him. He rose up, plunged forward into her, and was instantly encompassed by sweet warmth and then her firm legs clamped around his back. "Come . . . come . . . God, come," Janet breathed as she pumped feverishly. She screamed out as his hands cupped her round rear and pushed with her. "Yes, yes, more . . . oh, God, more, more . . . Fargo . . . Fargo," she cried out with chunky little body feverishly pumping faster and faster, and he heard her making little laughing sounds of pure joy with his every thrust. She never stopped pumping as her thighs tightened around him and he heard her breath grow shallow, become a hoarse scream. "Yes, yes . . . now, oh, God, it's happening . . . now, now, oh God," Janet screamed, and her full, high breasts thrust upward, her legs a soft vise around him, and her body pumping, pumping. He felt himself erupt with her, carried by her fevered urgency, and she screamed as she felt him expand, throb, pulsate inside her.

"Oh, Fargo . . . oh, good God," Janet whispered hoarsely, and fell back with her eyes closed, her little pubic mound still rising and falling until finally she lay quietly, only tiny sounds of pure happiness bubbling from her. Function sometimes follows form, he found himself thinking as he lay beside her: her lovemaking was as pugnacious as her face and figure—and as exciting in its own way, an explosion of sheer sensuous energy.

She turned to him after a few minutes and her tongue

licked his chest, tracing tiny circles around his nipples. He felt her hands move along his powerful body, touching, enjoying, exploring. She found his resting organ and caressed and stroked it into instant response. She closed her hands around him to feel the surging pulsations grow in strength and Fargo heard her little laughing sounds of excitement and joy. "Oh, yes, yes, yes," she murmured as he grew for her into a throbbing, wanting spear. Janet moved quickly, swung her body over his, and she was pumping again even before she was astride him. She wriggled, twisted, finally found him, and plunged herself down in a sweet impalement that made her gasp out in ecstasy. Once again, when she screamed in that moment of moments, her firm, rounded little body never slowed its pumping, not until rapture receded and ecstasy ebbed, the senses finally bowing to saturation. She turned on her side, and one leg draped across his body, she slept at once and he joined her in slumber until the midmorning sun streamed through the window.

He woke and she half-rose, rubbed sleep from her eyes, the round, high breasts deliciously firm, her body shimmering with latent energy. "You're a damn firecracker," he muttered. "No wonder that temper of yours explodes so damn quick."

"It all hangs together, I guess." She shrugged. "But a firecracker doesn't go off by itself. It needs something to light it."

"Guess so." He laughed as he rose to his feet. "Get dressed. I've a few other things to light today, but first you're going to take me to that little cabin."

She nodded happily and he made coffee as she washed and dressed.

The sun was bright and the air cold when he brought

the Ovaro and the roan out of the stable. "Got any thread?" he asked Janet as she started from the house and she returned to bring him a spool of black cotton thread. He closed the stable door and stretched the thread across the bottom of the doorway, using the edges of the splintered wood to hold it in place. "Just to play safe," he said.

They rode across the layer of snow still on the ground, though it had begun to melt in irregular streaks. His eyes swept the low hills to each side and scanned the clusters of red cedars and alders. His falcon's vision espied the horseman under the branches at the edge of the cedars and Janet heard his grunt of acknowledgment.

"What is it?" she asked.

"Somebody up there in the cedars. Tilden's watchdog, more than likely," Fargo said. "Just keep riding on."

Janet forced herself not to glance at the distant trees, and they rode tandem over a low hill down into an almost hidden ravine lined with bitternut on both sides of a little stream that coursed down its center. The cabin suddenly appeared at the bottom of the little ravine and Janet halted to stare at it for a moment before she dismounted. "Brings back memories," she murmured.

He went inside with her. A cot lined one wall, two three-legged stools and an old chest were against another. A pile of firewood still rested in one corner, and the stone fireplace was clean and ready to use. He walked from the cabin and looked at it again from the outside. A corner of the roof logs had been gnawed away, but the corner fit was still tight. He took in the bushes alongside the cabin and the bitternut that grew near the rear corners. The little stream turned to flow past the left side of the cabin and Fargo let his eyes slowly scan the surroundings once more.

"It'll do fine," he told Janet as she stepped from the cabin. "Let's get back."

"Do you mind telling me what you're planning to do?" she asked.

"Later," he said curtly.

They mounted their horses and rode up to the mouth of the ravine.

"Do you think Tilden's man followed us?" Janet asked.

"No, too much open land. But I'll bet he takes off after our tracks when we get back. They'll be easy enough to follow with the snow still on the ground."

"So what kind of a hiding place will the cabin be, then?" Janet frowned.

"Just the kind I'll want." He laughed and sent the Ovaro into a canter. When they returned to the house, he swung from the saddle and dropped to one knee at the stable door. The thread was unbroken and he snapped it as he pulled the door open. "No visitors," he said with satisfaction. "I'll be back later. You stay here, keep those calves in the stable, and just lay low."

She nodded, her hazel eyes watching as he climbed onto the Ovaro. "Be careful," she said. "And save some energy."

He laughed and sent the Ovaro into a fast canter. He rode steadily and reached the Farrow ranch in mid-afternoon. Abram Farrow walked carefully toward the house from the nearest corral as Fargo rode to a halt. The man greeted him with a smile and Fargo saw Alberta appear in the doorway. She helped Abram up the few steps, but her eyes stayed on Fargo. "Wondered where you've been," Abram said to the big man. "Thought any about staying on?"

"Some," Fargo answered, and followed him and Alberta into the house. "Can't do it. I'll be heading out today," he said, and saw Alberta search his face. He tossed her a pleasant smile. "Owen around?" he asked. "I'd like to say good-bye to him."

"He's inside," Alberta said crossly as she led the way into the living room.

Fargo saw Owen look up from where he lounged on the settee. His red-rimmed eyes narrowed as he saw the big man come into the room.

"Just stopped to say good-bye," Fargo announced.

"I thought you'd stay awhile longer, if only to help Janet some more," Alberta said with acid in her voice.

Fargo smiled at her. "No reason to. She's got her two young calves back. She found them under a rock ledge none the worse for wear." Alberta stared at him and Owen reacted as though he'd been slapped in the face. "She's gone off to hole up someplace where she'll be safe," Fargo added.

"Hole up someplace?" Alberta frowned and Fargo noted Owen watched him closely.

"Someplace only she knows about, she told me," he answered, and saw Owen blink and Alberta's eyes fill with racing thoughts. "She's going to stay there and let those two calves grow some and one day they'll be the start of her breeding program," he went on. "Much obliged for everything." He nodded directly to Abram and tossed Alberta a wide smile. "You, too," he said as she stared at him with eyes of lavender stone.

"I'll walk to the door with you," she said, and strode out of the house with him. "No more questions? No more suspicions?" she said as he mounted the Ovaro.

He shrugged. "No need for them. I'm pulling out. I don't care much what happens here," he said, and his glance took in Owen in the doorway, within easy earshot.

Fargo sent the Ovaro trotting slowly from the ranch

and he whistled softly, increasing speed only when he was out of sight of the ranch. Dusk was sliding its purple blanket across the land and night had followed when he reached Janet's house. She opened the door with the old Hawken in hand. "You have visitors?" He frowned.

"No, just playing safe," she said. "You do everything you wanted to do?"

"Yep," he said as he sat down. "I told everyone you'd gotten your calves back and were going to hole up someplace only you knew about."

Janet stared at him in disbelief. "What'd you do that for?" she protested. "They'll figure out where I'd be going to hide and you said Tilden's man probably followed our tracks. I'll be a target again."

"You can't find the snake, you let the snake find you," Fargo said calmly. "They also think I've pulled up stakes. Somebody will come looking for you there, this time to finish it once and for all. Only you won't be there alone."

Her hazel eyes were grave. "What if you don't stop them?"

"Then, honey, neither of us will have to wonder what the weather will be like tomorrow," he told her. "Now, you go hitch up that wagon and put the calves in it and go to that cabin of yours."

"Where will you be?"

"Around." He grinned at her.

"Think they'll come tonight?" she asked.

"Good chance of it. Somebody's going to be real anxious," Fargo said.

"Tilden," she muttered.

"Somebody," he said. "Get moving." He settled down in a corner of the room and Janet went to the stable. She left the door open and he could hear her getting the wagon ready. When she came back, her face was grave again.

"I'm ready. I tied the roan up behind the wagon."

"Douse the fire here. Turn out the lamp and close the door when you leave," he said.

"You think somebody's watching?" she asked apprehensively.

"Probably not, but I'm taking no chances. Somebody might stop by here to check out the place. I want them to see a place closed down," he told her.

"When do I see you again?" she asked.

"When it's time," he said.

She came to him, clung to him as she knelt down for a long moment and let her lips linger on his. She pushed herself to her feet finally, the hazel eyes filled with anxiety, and she hurried from the house, pulling the door shut behind her. He listened to the wagon roll away, waited a spell longer, and got to his feet in the blackness of the room. He paused at the door, listened, and opened it enough to slip outside. He climbed onto the Ovaro and rode from the house in the opposite direction Janet had taken. Anyone watching for tracks would see that and figure he'd stopped to say good-bye. He made a wide circle in the night and felt the winter wind stab at him; when he finished the circle, he was near the little ravine. The tracks of the wagon were clear on the ground where snow still lay in patches. When he reached the mouth of the ravine, he dismounted and led the Ovaro deep into the bitternut that lined the area; he tied the reins to a low branch and made his way back to the ravine on foot.

He moved down the incline with the silence of a cougar on the hunt and halted when he came in sight of the cabin. Smoke spiraled from the chimney, and reflected firelight touched the lone window. She had pulled the wagon to one side and taken the calves in with her. Fargo crept to one side of the ravine where a low-branched bitternut edged its branches over the path that led down the center. He sank down in the deep shadows of the tree and settled himself. Waiting, unlike with most men, didn't fill him with mounting impatience. He had learned to wait as the hawk waits, aware that stillness was only another form of action, and he sat as calmly after the first long hours as when he'd settled down. He could see the little cabin. The fire had all but gone out; only a wisp of smoke came from the chimney and Janet had gone to sleep. The soft bleat of one of the calves carried through the silence to where he sat.

He had his head back against the tree trunk when he caught the sound, the slow-footsteps of a horse. He was in a crouch at once, his ears straining. More than one horse, he muttered silently, but they were moving too slowly for him to tell how many. He faded back into the trees and moved down toward the cabin on silent steps, halting in the brush at the side of the cabin. By now the horses had drifted apart enough for him to count hoof-beats. Three horses, he counted, and the sound suddenly stopped, leaving only silence in the near blackness of the little ravine. Fargo stayed crouched low, his ears straining to catch any sound. But the silence remained and he suddenly saw the first pink streak touching the sky and understood the silence. They were taking no chances. They waited for the first gray light. They wanted no mistakes.

Fargo stayed motionless, hardly breathing, and watched the sky begin to lighten with surprising speed. The pink streak broadened in the sky and the gray dawn dipped down to touch the land. The little cabin took on soft clarity, and as Fargo watched, two men on foot, each with a rifle in hand, came into view. He cursed silently. There had been three horses. One figure was behind and out of sight. He swept the ravine again with a measured glance but spotted no one else. The third figure was not moving back in the deep brush across from him. He cursed again as he brought his eyes back to the two men. They were moving to the door of the cabin together, their rifles at their waists. Goddamn, Fargo cursed silently. They were going to crash the door and spray the room and everything in it with bullets.

He drew the big Colt, and his lips pulled back in frustration. He had to stop them. The third figure, hidden in the brush, would see. There'd be no surprise, but he had no choice. He raised the Colt and took aim as the two men rushed at the door. He fired. The man nearest him suddenly had only an explosion of red where the side of his face had been. The second one spun in surprise, hardly six inches from the cabin door, and took Fargo's second shot full in the chest. The heavy slug sent him sailing backward as though he'd been kicked by a mule.

Fargo's eyes went to the brush across from him in the gray dawn light. Nothing moved, but he saw the cabin door flung open out of the corner of his eye as Janet burst out in a thin cotton nightdress. "Goddamn," he muttered as she halted, eyes round as she stared at the two still figures on the ground. Fargo let out a sigh of frustration; it was too late now. She was outside, in full view, and he wanted to fan her little ass for it.

Fargo lifted his voice and called across the clearing in front of the cabin. "Come out, Carver," he said. "Try to run for it and I'll cut you down."

Ed Carver's voice answered with icy calmness. "I've a

bead on her, Fargo. I'll shoot her right between those
nice hazel eyes unless you throw your gun out," the man
said.

Fargo swore at the world, and mostly at Janet Farrow.
He waited, tried to find a way out, but Carver's voice
only affirmed what he knew. There was no way out.

"Five seconds, Fargo, or she gets it," the man said.

Fargo rose, threw his gun out, and stepped from the
brush, pausing only to glare at Janet. The diminutive
figure moved out of the brush across from him, a small
pocket pistol in his hand, a rimfire French-made gam-
bler's pistol but deadly enough at close range.

Janet stared at the little man with shock in her face as
Carver moved closer. The big Colt lay less than a half-
dozen inches from Fargo's boot and Carver gestured to
it. "Kick it over here," he ordered.

Fargo drew his foot back and kicked, twisted at the last
moment, and sent the gun skidding into the bushes.
Carver's eyes followed it for an instant, a reflex action
Fargo had counted on. He dived forward, a low, downward lunge that sent him into the little man just above
the ankles. He heard the small explosion of the pistol as
the shot went over his head and Carver hit the ground.
Fargo started to bring his arms up, but the little man
kicked out with his short legs, knocked Fargo's arm
aside, and rolled out of his grip. The dapper little figure
was on his feet instantly, and though the pistol was on
the ground, Ed Carver drew a knife from his pearl-gray
vest.

Fargo pulled himself up into a half-crouch, remembering how he had seen Ed Carver outfight a man more
than twice his size and finally knife him to death. He
moved carefully, feinted a blow, and saw the little man
move with the quickness of a dragonfly. Ed Carver held

the knife ready to plunge into his target and Fargo moved in again. He had three times the reach on the little man and he tried to use it with a hard left jab. Carver slipped the blow effortlessly and Fargo followed with two more, hard, fast jabs that would have hit right on target normally, but again the small man easily slipped the blows.

Fargo pressed forward and knew he had to avoid the mistake of getting frustrated or careless. Ed Carver was no ordinary man. He was a killer in tailored clothes with the prowess of a cornered weasel. Fargo thought of trying to draw his throwing knife but he knew he'd never get it from the holster alive. He had to fight the little man barehanded, to somehow catch him with one solid blow that would end it. He moved in at Carver again and saw the man's icy smile. He tried two left feints and followed with a right uppercut. Carver danced away from the feints and pulled back from the uppercut. With the quickness of diamondback's strike he slashed with the blade while Fargo's arm was still upraised at the follow-through and Fargo felt the sharp pain along his forearm. He twisted away as Carver slashed again with lightninglike speed. Fargo felt the blade rip the skin of his shoulder.

Aware that uppercuts were an invitation to death, Fargo moved forward again. He swung a left hook, barely managing to pull his bleeding forearm back in time to avoid an upward thrust of the knife. He pulled away from another slash, tried another left hook and a vicious right cross after it, but saw the little figure dance away on the balls of his feet. Fargo started a lunge, feinted with his body to the left, and threw a right. The blow grazed Carver's chin but he came up under it with a sideways slash of the blade and Fargo felt the sharp pain in his side. The demonic little man was too fast. Ed Carver intended to slice him to ribbons, Fargo realized, and then plunge the knife in to finish the battle when his foe was weakened and slowed further.

The man was fast, clever, and crafty, but he'd shown one thing more: he never held back when he saw an opening. He counted on his speed and dexterity to strike and get away. But he struck whenever he saw the chance. Fargo threw a series of blows, staying enough away to avoid Carver's counterthrusts, and then he started to feint and move backward. He let his left jabs grow slower and the little man almost laughed as he slipped the blows. Fargo lunged, feinted again, and started to twist away from a countering slash of the blade. He let his feet fall over each other and faked a fall, going down on one knee, off balance.

Carver leapt in immediately with a slashing blow and Fargo turned his already ripped shoulder and felt the knife tear into almost the same spot. But this time he brought a crushing right up as Carver, overanxious, thought he had his chance to end it. The blow caught Ed Carver on the point of the jaw and Fargo heard his jawbone crack. The little figure rose from the ground and catapulted into the air. As Carver came down, Fargo lashed out with a looping left hook and caught him alongside the head as he toppled forward. Ed Carver's neck twisted grotesquely as his head spun around. He landed on the ground and lay still, looking not unlike a handsomely dressed doll whose head had been turned almost backward.

Fargo pulled himself to his feet, dripping blood from too many places, and felt Janet pulling him into the cabin. "I've ointment and arrowroot compound," she said as she tore his shirt off and made it into bandages.

"I'm sorry," she said as she worked on him. "I just ran out the door. I didn't think."

"I know. You reacted," he said. "But it's over."

"You knew it was Ed Carver. How?" she asked. "How did you know it wasn't Barnaby Tilden?"

"You said it yourself. You were nothing to him, not family, not friends, nothing. He had no reason to hold back. If it had been Tilden, he'd have gone at you right away. He's that kind of man. That's what kept bothering me about him. Whoever was behind it held back for a while, picking off your hand, trying to stop you by killing the calves. If it were Tilden, he wouldn't have done it that way."

"But Carver had no reason to hold back. I was nothing to him," Janet said.

"He had a reason called Owen. His books will show that Owen was into him for a small fortune. A few more months of losses and he could take the ranch as a settlement. He wasn't about to let you wreck all that for him, but he had to think about Owen. If he'd just killed you, Owen might have come apart, maybe even have run to the sheriff."

"Owen was part of what he was doing?" Janet said.

"Yes, he wanted you stopped, too. But he agreed only because Carver had convinced him he'd do it without hurting you."

"Poor Owen, sucked in by his own weaknesses." Janet murmured as she finished the last bandage.

"I knew Owen would tell him you had the calves back and, like a fool, still believe Carver would keep playing it his way. But Carver would know he'd wasted enough time and go after you to finish it once and for all. He probably had a story all ready to give Owen."

"What's that make Owen?" she asked. "A conspirator?"

"Not to kill you. It makes him just what you said he was: a weakling and a desperate fool," Fargo said.

"How'd you know it wasn't Alberta? She's no weakling and she had no love for me," Janet asked.

"But she was afraid to do more than try to get rid of the calves. If she did more and anything happened to you, there was always the chance Abram might find out. She wasn't ready to take that chance. She still had the hope without the power," Fargo said.

"I feel sick," Janet said. "I want to go back to my place and shut them all out."

"Good idea. Get the wagon," Fargo said. "We'll pick up the Ovaro along the way."

"Can you ride that bouncy wagon?" she asked.

"Sure," he said. "I hurt a little, but none of the cuts are deep. I bounce back quickly."

"Good," she said. "When we get back to my place, all you have to do is lie still."

"Think you can do all the rest by yourself?" He grinned.

"Now who's jumping to conclusions," she said.

"Was I wrong?" he asked.

"No," she murmured. "Let's hurry."

"That's the best idea you've had since I met you," he said as he closed one hand around a firm, high breast. "Let's hurry."

LOOKING FORWARD!

**The following is the opening section
from the next novel in the exciting
Trailsman Series from Signet:**

**The Trailsman #42:
*RENEGADE COMMAND***

*1861—Sioux country, where Fargo
finds himself caught between a Sioux
chieftain's fury and the treacherous cowardice
of his renegade command . . .*

At first glance the fort below—Fort Alexander—looked perfectly normal. As Fargo sat astride his powerful black-and-white Ovaro, the hot July sun resting like a welcome hand on his shoulder, his keen eyes took in the ragged palisades and log quarters, the dusty parade ground, and the low profile of the sutler's store. Fargo was pleased. Before this night was out he would be sleeping under army blankets, and more than likely, this would come after he and the major had plundered his reserves of bourbon.

That was Fargo's first, momentary impression.

An instant later, however, his sharp eyes caught something that sent an uneasy chill up his spine. A troop of cavalry was riding into the fort through the gates— without challenge. Watching them dismount in front of their barracks, Fargo was astonished at their ragged, careless bearing. Some were not wearing their campaign hats and others had not even bothered to put on their cavalry tunics, their broad yellow braces standing out clearly against their pale underwear.

And then it became what Fargo did not see—the lack of brisk, purposeful activity about the fort, the deserted parade grounds, the scant livestock in the corrals. Nor were there any horses standing at the hitch rail in front of the sutler's store. No women were visible, and on the clotheslines behind the enlisted men's quarters, not a single stitch of clothing was hanging.

Fargo put the pinto down the steep slope on an angle. Despite his size, the powerful Ovaro carried him with deceptive ease. Dressed in a buckskin shirt, jacket, and pants, and wearing a wide-brimmed hat, Fargo was a big, broad-shouldered man with hair as black as a raven's wing, a sharp, powerful blade of a nose, and eyes the color of a lake under a blue sky.

It had not rained in weeks and the tall grass was scorched yellow, the trees drooping listlessly in the windless, ovenlike heat. But Fargo was not thinking of the weather at the moment. He was wondering anxiously what had happened to Major Hollister's command. Fargo knew Major Hollister as a no-nonsense, spit-and-polish disciplinarian, a stickler for details and a strategist who was already a match for the local Sioux chieftain Black Feather.

The only thing Fargo could figure was that something must have happened to the major.

Fargo gained the flat and rode across a shallow stream, heading for the entrance to the fort. Unlike so many of the other army forts in the region, which were for the most part a careless sprawl of buildings set out on a flat with little or no barrier to the hostiles, Fort Alexander was surrounded by a rough but solid log palisade. It had been called Fort Henry in the days of the American Fur Company, and the fur company's builders had taken advantage of the heavily timbered hills nearby to surround the fort with a palisade in order to protect their stores of beaver, bear, and buffalo hides.

The gates sagged open ahead of Fargo. Riding through them into the fort, he pulled his pinto up and looked around. The few troopers he saw watched him warily, and not one greeted him cordially. Across the parade ground one trooper hurried into the headquarters building. He moved furtively almost, glancing back at Fargo just before he disappeared.

Fargo nudged the pinto forward, and before he finished crossing the parade ground, an officer and two others stepped from the headquarters building and halted on the low porch to wait for him. When Fargo reached the three men, he noticed that the officer in charge was not a major, but a captain, a pale, slack-faced fellow with watery eyes and sandy hair. He needed a shave and his uniform was in even worse disrepair than that of his sergeant.

Fargo pulled up and dismounted.

"My name's Skye Fargo," he told the captain, dropping the pinto's reins over the hitch rail. "Where's Major Hollister?"

"He pulled out."

"Pulled out?"

"There's a war on back East. Or ain't you heard?"

"I heard, Captain."

"So we're all that's left to keep the peace hereabouts." The captain smiled coldly. "I'm Captain Edward Blaine. You're welcome to stay the night."

"Thank you, Captain."

"What's your business in the area, Fargo? This ain't very friendly country."

"I'm looking for a man—maybe two men—last seen headed this way."

"You a bounty hunter?"

"No. I just want the man."

"You don't care about any bounty."

Fargo nodded.

"Well, outside of a few settlers passing through, you're the first stranger my men and I have seen in weeks. You won't find them two in this fort."

"Wasn't expecting I would." Fargo glanced over at the sutler's store. It looked quite deserted and Fargo had been looking forward to wetting his whistle in there. "Did the sutler pull out with the major?"

Capt. Blaine nodded.

"I'm sure sorry to hear that. I'm dry as sawdust."

"A word of advice," Capt. Blaine told him. "The store is boarded up for a reason. Stay away from it. Everything in there's army property—including the rum."

"I'm not a thief, Captain."

"Just so we understand each other."

Capt. Blaine turned to his sergeant. "Take Mister Fargo's horse to the stable, Sergeant, then show him to his quarters."

The captain and his remaining orderly turned and walked back inside the headquarters building. Leading his pinto, Fargo followed the sergeant across the compound to the stables, alongside of which had been built a series of low mud-and-log buildings. Evidently these were the quarters the captain had in mind for Fargo.

After seeing to the pinto, the big, red-faced noncom led Fargo from the stables and showed him into a cheerless room furnished with only a broken chest of drawers and a single dusty army cot.

Fargo turned to the sergeant. "Tell me, Sergeant, what do you think of the captain?"

The sergeant eyed Fargo warily. "What do you mean?"

"To my way of thinking, he's a pretty slack commanding officer."

"We like him just fine."

"Do you, now?"

"And you'd do well to keep your opinions to yourself around here."

"I'll remember that, Sergeant."

"See that you do." The sergeant turned and left.

Stepping to the door of his drab quarters, Fargo watched the sergeant move along the boardwalk on his way back to the headquarters building. The big fellow slouched. His hat was pushed far back on his head. His shirt, filthy, had been open at the collar. Fargo looked away from the sergeant and studied the other troopers moving listlessly about the compound. They were no better dressed and walked with no more pride or discipline than did their sergeant or commanding officer.

Fargo was unimpressed. He had little confidence in this command's ability to offer solid protection for the few settlers passing through. And as for keeping Black Feather and his Sioux in line, these men would be hopeless. Fargo promised himself to push on, first thing in the morning. This fort reminded him of a house of cards waiting to collapse.

While stowing his gear under the cot a moment later, Fargo heard the rumble of wagon wheels and the high, nervous whinny of horses driven too hard. Glancing out the window, he saw two wagons charging through the gate into the fort, a tall, dark-haired woman handling the first team, a grizzled old timer Fargo vaguely remembered from somewhere driving the second team. This second wagon had its canvas top burned through in spots and a large piece of it was flapping in the wind like a broken wing. It was obvious what was up. The wagons were fleeing from hostiles. Black Feather, more than likely.

As the wagons rattled past the fort's sagging gates, two troopers ran to close them, while other troopers—including the captain and his sergeant—hurried over to where the wagons had pulled to a halt. Fargo stepped out of his quarters, peering more closely at the older bearded fellow who had been driving the second wagon. As Fargo watched him, he jumped to the ground to help the woman down.

And then Fargo knew who the man was. Jeb Dugan!

With a quick, pleased smile, Fargo hurried out to greet his old friend. He had aged considerably these past ten years; it was his white head and white beard that had momentarily confounded Fargo. But there was no mistaking Jeb's deep voice or the way he carried his still-powerful, heavily muscled figure.

"Jeb, you old son of a bitch," Fargo cried, brushing past the captain and the sergeant to cuff the new arrival on his shoulder.

"Fargo," Jeb cried, equally surprised and delighted. "What the hell you doin' here?"

"I just rode in an hour ago."

Jeb sobered then. "You still lookin' for them varmints?"

"Reckon so."

"You gettin' any closer."

"There's only two left now."

Jeb nodded and turned to the girl standing beside him. "This here's Skye Fargo, Theresa." Glancing back at Fargo, Jeb said, "Meet Theresa Wayland, Fargo."

Fargo touched the brim of his hat to Theresa and nodded. She returned his greeting with a barely perceptible nod in return. It was clear she was close to collapse and Fargo saw a dismal, naked despair in her eyes.

"I just got through plucking Theresa out of Black Feather's clutches," Jeb explained. "I wasn't so lucky with the others, though. And them redskins've still got my horses and skins."

"Would you like to explain what happened, mister?" the captain asked, obviously irritated at the way Jeb had left off his account the moment he saw Fargo.

"Sure, Captain," Jeb said. "Sorry, I broke off like that. Ain't seen this here friend of mine in a coon's age. Like I was telling you, Black Feather and his braves were chasing after me for my skins when they came onto this here wagon train. They left me for the wagons, but I managed to rescue Miss Wayland here and steal that other wagon."

"What happened to the others?" Fargo asked.

Theresa spoke up then. "My father was taken captive. So was the family in the other wagon."

"How many in that other party?"

"A man and wife," Jeb said. "And two young 'uns."

"How old were the kids?"

"The boy was eight, the girl six."

Fargo frowned. He did not like the sound of that.

"You know what happened to the family?" the captain asked.

"We ain't sure," Jeb said. "Last I heard, the husband was hollerin' pretty loud. The Indians didn't take kindly to the way he shot up the attacking war party."

"Were the children hurt during the attack?" Fargo asked the woman.

She shook her head numbly, her eyes bleak. "I don't know," she managed. "I am not sure."

"Did the Sioux follow you here?" the captain asked Jeb.

"Last time I looked."

The captain began issuing orders to the sergeant, who in turn took charge of the preparations. The troopers came running, some posting themselves near the gate, others mounting to the rickety catwalks high on the palisades. Still a ragtag, uninspiring lot, they were moving now with some urgency. The threat of hostiles had a way of making even those sorry specimens concentrate powerfully.

The captain turned to Theresa. "If you will allow me, Miss Wayland, I'll escort you to your quarters. I warn you, though, they ain't much."

"That's all right," said Theresa. "I'll stay here—in my wagon. There's still a bed inside and most of my belongings."

"As you wish." The captain stalked off.

"Well, now," Jeb said, watching Blaine depart. "Ain't *he* a friendly son of a bitch?"

"No, he ain't, and that's the pure truth of it."

"If you'll excuse me, gentlemen," said Theresa. "I find I am exhausted." She turned then and clambered wearily up into her wagon.

"Don't you worry none about that black-hearted Injun chief, Miss Wayland," Jeb told her. "Fargo and me'll keep an eye out for you."

"Thank you," she managed, disappearing into her wagon.

A moment later, as the two men started to move off, they heard Theresa's muffled sobbing. She was now having to contemplate alone the miserable fate of her father and those friends she had traveled with these long months past.

Black Feather and a small band of Sioux appeared not long after at the far end of the flat. Fargo and Jeb hastened up the ladders to the scaffold, rifles loaded and ready, and took their places beside the troopers. But the Sioux pulled up when they saw where the wagon tracks led. Then, raising their rifles high, they let out a few piercing war cries and peeled back into the timber.

The scare over, the troopers streamed back down the

ladders and immediately lapsed into their former disorderly state. Laughing in relief and digging one another with their elbows, they trailed off to their barracks—some of them already unsteady on their feet as they pulled on the flasks of whiskey they rescued from their back pockets.

Watching them, Fargo shook his head. "I don't like it," he told Jeb.

"What do you mean?"

"There's something wrong here."

"You feel it too, do you?"

"From the moment I rode in."

"Well," drawled Jeb, "they ain't a pretty bunch—and that's for sure. But I'm mighty grateful all the same."

"Why?"

"Because this here fort's open and fully manned. It was a gamble of mine that paid off."

The two had been on their way to Fargo's quarters. Fargo halted at Jeb's words and turned to face him, a frown on his face. "A gamble? What do you mean?"

"Hell, Fargo, there warn't supposed to be any troopers here."

"How come?"

"The word I got from Fort Platte was Major Hollister had done pulled out his entire command." Jeb shook his head. "I'm sure as hell grateful the army changed its mind."

Inside Fargo a vague doubt became a certainty as many odd facts and observations fell into place. He resumed walking toward his quarters.

"Maybe the army didn't change its mind, Jeb."

"Now, what in tarnation do you mean by that?"

"Jeb, I don't think the army had a thing to do with these men being here—or assigning Captain Blaine as their commanding officer. Hell, to begin with, I don't even think Blaine *is* an officer."

"What's that? Not an officer?"

"You heard me."

"Jesus, Fargo, do you know what you're sayin'?"

They entered Fargo's quarters. Fargo closed the door, went to the window, and looked out across the compound, his eye on the headquarters building. "I know what I'm saying," Fargo replied. "It sounds crazy, I know. But I got a hunch these here troopers are deserters, renegades. As soon as the major pulled out, they moved into the post and took it over."

Jeb scratched his head meditatively. "I got to admit, you got the captain pegged. He sure as hell don't look or act like no officer to me. And he keeps a mean and sloppy post. But supposin' you're right? How're we goin' to find out for sure?"

"A little while ago," Fargo replied, "the captain warned me away from the sutler's store. I think as soon as it gets dark enough—say around midnight—maybe you and I ought to find out why."

Jeb grunted assent. "You're on, Fargo."

The board groaned as Fargo bent it back, pulling the carelessly hammered nails out with it. With a sudden crack, it broke free and Jeb got a firm grip on the second board and pulled that out as well, giving them access to the store's narrow back door. Fargo took the knob and tried to open it. It was locked.

"Stand back," whispered Jeb. The big trapper placed

his right foot on the door, just under the knob—and thrust forward. The lock held, but the doorjamb splintered and the door sagged open.

The two men moved cautiously into the sutler's store. Fargo found a lantern and lit it. They came to a storeroom and pulled up just outside it.

"Oh, bloody Jesus!" Jeb exclaimed. "That smell!"

"Someone's in there," Fargo agreed. "But he's sure as hell ripe."

Holding handkerchiefs over their faces, the two men pushed open the door to the storeroom, then turned away, hardly able to keep their stomachs from heaving up their contents. Holding the lantern over the dead man lying sprawled on the floor, Fargo saw his blood-stained apron still tied about his waist, his woolen shirt with rolled-up sleeves, and he knew at once who it was.

The sutler hadn't left with the major, after all.

"What's that?"

Both men pulled back and listened. A steady, agitated thumping was coming from the other side of the store. It resembled the sound a boot or shoe would make if it were kicking continually at a wall or door.

"Close off the storeroom," Fargo told Jeb as he hurried into the front of the store, skirted the counter, and headed for another door leading to the granary.

Holding the lantern high with one hand, he pulled it open and found himself looking down at the disheveled bound-and-gagged figure of a young woman in her twenties. Her dress was torn from ankle to hip, and her blouse had been ripped off her shoulders. She was close to being naked, and her pale figure was covered with bruises. Putting the lantern down beside her, Fargo untied the gag. Tears of frustration and rage coursed down her face.

"Whoever you are, take me!" She panted hysterically. "Do what you will. But don't let that man near me again!"

"What man?" Jeb asked.

"The captain!"

"Easy now, easy," said Fargo, taking out his bowie and slicing through the rope that bound her ankles and wrists. "We ain't going to do nothing to you."

"And neither is that captain," Jeb said, leaning over Fargo's shoulder. "Not after we get through with that bastard."

Behind them, the front door slammed open. Fargo spun to see the sergeant pause in the doorway, the large navy Colt in his hand leveled at the three of them. The gun was cocked and there was a pleased grin on his face as his finger tightened on the trigger.

Fargo still had the bowie in his hand. In one single powerful upward stroke, he flung it at the sergeant. The knife left his palm on a flat trajectory and sliced into the man's chest, the long blade slipping between his ribs to bury itself hilt-deep into his heart. With only a slight, barely audible gasp, the sergeant sagged to the floor, plunging forward onto the knife, driving its blade in still deeper.

Jeb hurried to the sergeant's side and flung him over.

"He's a gone beaver," Jeb told Fargo, pulling the knife free.

Fargo took the knife from Jeb and looked back at the girl. Her face was a stark white as she stared wide-eyed at

Excerpt from RENEGADE COMMAND

the dead man. Then she looked at Fargo, the color rushing back into her face.

"You killed him!"

"I had no choice."

"You think I care? He was going to take me to the captain."

"That means Blaine is waiting for you now."

"Yes."

"And where would he be waiting?"

"In the headquarters building. He sleeps in his office."

"Maybe it's time I gave the captain a visit," Fargo told Jeb. Then he looked back at the girl. "What's your name?"

"Angelique. My father runs this store."

Fargo winced inwardly and glanced quickly up at Jeb. Angelique pushed herself to a sitting position. In her state she was unaware of how scantily she was clad and of its possible effect on Fargo or Jeb.

"Have you seen my father?" the girl asked anxiously. "He's a big man with red hair. He must be worried about me. I must go to him."

Without replying to her, Fargo looked quickly up at Jeb. "Take care of Angelique," he said, "I want a chat with this captain."

"You sure you won't need me?"

"I'd rather you stay with Angelique. It might not be a bad idea if you took her to Miss Wayland's wagon."

"Good idea," Jeb said, helping the girl to her feet.

As Jeb and the girl slipped out into the darkness, Fargo wiped off his bowie's blade and cut back out through the rear of the store.

*   *   *

There was a thin sliver of light visible under the door to the captain's office. Fargo knocked once, softly.

"That you, Sergeant?"

Fargo mumbled something.

Footsteps approached the door, and a second later it was pulled open. Fargo pushed into the dim room, the nuzzle of his Colt thrusting deep into the captain's soft belly.

"Angelique isn't coming tonight," Fargo said.

The captain was dismayed. Dressed only in his filthy long johns, he looked desperately around for his weapon—a Colt resting on his desk. Fargo reached over for it and thrust it into his belt.

"Now suppose you explain what's going on here," Fargo told Blaine, pushing him roughly down into the chair behind his desk.

"I don't have to explain nothin' to you," Blaine said defiantly. "You can't touch me. Fire that gun and my men will be in here before you holster your weapon. You're my prisoner—you and that old mountain man. Black Feather's waitin' for you outside the fort, and my men have you inside." He reached out for Fargo's gun. "You better let me have that."

Fargo slammed the barrel hard against the side of Blaine's face. The force of the blow nearly lifted the man from his chair. His hand held dazedly up to his left cheekbone, he looked with sullen, watery eyes up at Fargo.

"You killed the sutler," Fargo told him.

Blaine swallowed, but made no effort to deny the accusation.

"Why?"

"He tried to kill me."

"He must have had a good reason."

Blaine laughed shortly, contemptuously. "He didn't want me to take his daughter. He said she was too good for me."

"From the looks of it, she is."

Still holding his chin, Blaine stormed, "I could have had you killed soon's you rode in here. You owe me. Now, put down that gun if you want to ride out of here alive."

"You're right. Maybe I can't get out of here alive if you sic your men on me. But you won't make it out alive, either. I won't have no choice in the matter, I'll just take you right along with me."

"Damn you! What do you want?"

"For starters, how many men you got?"

"Thirty-two."

"All of them deserters?"

"Most of them," Blaine admitted.

"And the rest?"

Blaine grinned coldly at Fargo. "I rescued them from the guardhouse."

"But they're troopers, every one of them."

"That's right."

"Good."

Blaine frowned. "What're you plannin', mister?"

"We're going on a campaign."

"A campaign?"

"That's right. I figure we've got the men here to teach Black Feather a lesson. Then we're getting out of here."

"You must be crazy. My men won't follow you."

"Sure, they will. If their scalps depend on it."

"I tell you you're crazy!"

"Stand up, Blaine."

"What for?"

"Do like I tell you."

Slowly, warily, Blaine got to his feet.

"Now, turn around."

"Damn you, Fargo," the man cried, without budging. "What are you going to do?"

Fargo grabbed Blaine's shoulder and spun him about. Then he brought the barrel of his Colt down on Blaine's head, knocking him unconscious. Catching the man before he sagged to the floor, Fargo slung his limp body over his shoulder and hurried from the office.

A moment later, still carrying his unconscious burden, Fargo was moving swiftly across the parade grounds toward the wagons barely visible in the dim starlight. He and Jeb still had much to do before this night was out, and if they were successful, they would find themselves with the happy task of leading a renegade command made up of murderers, malingerers, and outright deserters.

It was a wild scheme maybe, but it was the only way Fargo could think of to get those two kids—and maybe Theresa's father—out of the clutches of Black Feather's Sioux.

JOIN THE *TRAILSMAN* READERS' PANEL

Help us bring you more of the books you like by filling out this survey and mailing it in today.

1. Book Title: _____

   Book #: _____

2. Using the scale below, how would you rate this book on the following features? Please write in one rating from 0-10 for each feature in the spaces provided.

POOR	NOT SO GOOD		O.K.		GOOD		EXCEL-LENT
0	1	2	3	4	5	6	7	8	9	10

   RATING

   Overall opinion of book .... _____
   Plot/Story .... _____
   Setting/Location .... _____
   Writing Style .... _____
   Character Development .... _____
   Conclusion/Ending .... _____
   Scene on Front Cover .... _____

3. About how many western books do you buy for yourself each month? _____

4. How would you classify yourself as a reader of westerns? I am a ( ) light ( ) medium ( ) heavy reader.

5. What is your education?
   ( ) High School (or less) ( ) 4 yrs. college
   ( ) 2 yrs. college ( ) Post Graduate

6. Age _____ 7. Sex: ( ) Male ( ) Female

Please Print Name_____

Address_____

City _____ State _____ Zip _____

Phone # ( )_____

Thank you. Please send to New American Library, Research Dept., 1633 Broadway, New York, NY 10019.

Exciting Westerns by Jon Sharpe

(0451)

☐ THE TRAILSMAN #21: THE WHISKEY GUNS   (124898—$2.50)*
☐ THE TRAILSMAN #22: BORDER ARROWS   (125207—$2.50)*
☐ THE TRAILSMAN #23: THE COMSTOCK KILLERS   (125681—$2.50)*
☐ THE TRAILSMAN #24: TWISTED NOOSE   (126203—$2.50)*
☐ THE TRAILSMAN #25: MAVERICK MAIDEN   (126858—$2.50)*
☐ THE TRAILSMAN #26: WARPAINT RIFLES   (127757—$2.50)*
☐ THE TRAILSMAN #27: BLOODY HERITAGE   (128222—$2.50)*
☐ THE TRAILSMAN #28: HOSTAGE TRAIL   (128761—$2.50)*
☐ THE TRAILSMAN #29: HIGH MOUNTAIN GUNS   (129172—$2.50)*
☐ THE TRAILSMAN #30: WHITE SAVAGE   (129725—$2.50)*
☐ THE TRAILSMAN #31: SIX-GUN SOMBREROS   (130596—$2.50)*
☐ THE TRAILSMAN #32: APACHE GOLD   (131169—$2.50)*
☐ THE TRAILSMAN #33: RED RIVER REVENGE   (131649—$2.50)*
☐ THE TRAILSMAN #34: SHARPS JUSTICE   (131991—$2.50)*
☐ THE TRAILSMAN #35: KIOWA KILL   (132513—$2.50)*
☐ THE TRAILSMAN #36: THE BADGE   (132807—$2.50)*
☐ THE TRAILSMAN #37: VALLEY OF DEATH   (133374—$2.75)**
☐ THE TRAILSMAN #38: TOMAHAWK REVENGE   (134117—$2.75)**
☐ THE TRAILSMAN # 39: THE GRIZZLY MAN   (134842—$2.75)**

*Price is $2.95 in Canada
**Price is $3.25 in Canada.

**Buy them at your local
bookstore or use coupon
on next page for ordering.**

Ø

SIGNET Double Westerns You'll Enjoy